The Story of a Lie

The Story of a Lie

Robert Louis Stevenson

ET REMOTISSIMA PROPE

Hesperus Classics

Hesperus Classics
Published by Hesperus Press Limited
4 Rickett Street, London SW6 1RU
www.hesperuspress.com

The Story of a Lie first published in *New Quarterly Magazine*, 1879
'The Body Snatcher' first published in the *Pall Mall Gazette*, 1884

This collection first published by Hesperus Press Limited, 2008

Foreword © D.J. Taylor, 2008

Designed and typeset by Fraser Muggeridge studio
Printed in Jordan by Jordan National Press

ISBN: 978-1-84391-181-4

CONTENTS

FOREWORD

By the close of the Victorian era the gap between mass culture and high art – between the bestseller and the slim volume, the daily newspaper and the highbrow weekly – had grown into a chasm. As John Gross observes in his invaluable *The Rise and Fall of the Man of Letters*, if it was the age of Northcliffe and H.G. Wells, then it was also the age of the *Yellow Book*, the *Savoy*, the *Hobby Horse* and other exquisite trifles so obscure that they have vanished even from the bibliographies. Stevenson's vantage point on this process of cultural separation is more complicated than it might seem. On the one hand, mainstream critics who admired the dynamism of his action scenes fretted over the subtleties of his characterisation ('More claymores, less psychology,' as Andrew Lang famously demanded). On the other, many a grand literary eminence of the kind that Stevenson was occasionally disposed to mock signified warm approval. In his *Selected Letters of Robert Louis Stevenson*, Ernest Mehew prints a revealing exchange with Henry James, in which James talks of his 'hearty sympathy, charged with the assurance of my enjoyment of everything you write.' And James, it should be pointed out, was not simply being polite. That he regarded the author of *Treasure Island* as, in some sense, an ally is confirmed by some later remarks about the 'luxury' of encountering someone who '*does* write', as James put it, and 'who is really acquainted with that lovely art.'

'The Story of a Lie' and 'The Body Snatcher' are characteristic Stevenson productions: written on the hoof, against time, and for money – the latter for the *Pall Mall Gazette*'s Christmas number of 1884, the former in the course of a stormy Atlantic crossing five years before for the publishing house of

Kegan Paul's *New Quarterly Magazine* ('I worked… I worked,' runs a letter to W.E. Henley, 'and am now despatching a story as long as my arm to the vile Paul, all written in a slantindicular cabin with the table playing bob-cherry with the ink bottle.') Each comes crammed with the psychological detail that caused Lang to wonder whether he hadn't backed the wrong horse. 'The Story of a Lie', in particular, is a devious little parable about the need for absolute transparency in one's personal dealings. Dick Naseby is a strong-willed squire's son who falls out with his hot-tempered father on a point of principle. Travelling in France he comes across a shady-sounding ex-artist named Van Tromp, described as 'a dismal parasite upon the foreigner in Paris', who makes a living out of 'percentages' – that is, escorting his young friends to trades-men's shops and restaurants and taking a cut of the proceeds from their grateful proprietors. Dick, however, is man of the world enough to see through this imposture, whereupon their association lapses into a wary friendship.

Back in England, Dick falls in love with a young woman living with her aunt in a secluded cottage on the family estate. This, inevitably, is Van Tromp's daughter, not seen by him for many a year, and kept in provincial purdah by her exacting spinster aunt, Miss M'Glashan, on the plausible grounds that she '"couldn't save the mother – her that's dead – but the bairn!"' Encouraged by the tender object of his affections to dilate on her absent father's sterling qualities, his artistic talents, kindness, generosity and so forth, Dick offers a version of the old man that, while not exactly false, gives no idea of his real character. Their brief idyll is shattered by Van Tromp's unexpected return and a brisk series of emotional readjust-ments – not all of them wholly predictable – in the approved Victorian magazine style. Throughout, Van Tromp remains both the villain of the piece and the star of the show, one of those eternally disreputable, down-at-heel idlers in whom Stevenson always delights (Fettes in 'The Body Snatcher' is a variation on this theme), simultaneously brusque, flustered and calculating, first seen scribbling in a Parisian estaminet, where his vocal style is crisply paraphrased in an explanation of his drawing technique: '"I just dash them off like that. I – I dash them off."'

Van Tromp's signature mark, as Naseby soon discovers, is his poseur's love of role play. Relocated to the English country-side, and the society of his (initially) admiring daughter, he instantly abandons his *boulevardier*'s cane for a stout stick 'designed for rustic scenes', attends church, looks fondly on the daughter's choice of husband ('"Dick, I have been expect-ing this. Let us – let us go back to the Trevanion Arms and talk this matter out over a bottle"') while managing to betray him-self with both the brandy glass and savage irruptions of temper. There is a queer little scene in which Dick brings home a stack of artist's materials with which it is hoped that his prospective father-in-law can kick-start his career: far from welcoming these attentions the old man tells his daughter crossly not to '"interfere"'. Calmed down and mollified, he continues to add extra layers to the persona he has created for himself. He is '"an old Bohemain"', he proudly declares, who has '"cut society with a cut direct; I cut it when I was prosperous, and now I reap my reward and can cut it with dignity in my declension."' To say that Van Tromp bears a faint resemblance to one or two of Thackeray's broken-down old scamps – Costigan, say, in *Pendennis* – isn't to ignore either the air of seedy menace or the bracing economy of the sketch. The reader guesses far more about Van Tromp than Stevenson ever tells him, and an unseen rake's progress of squalid intrigues and seedy glamour stretches out behind him into the Paris backstreets. His real origins probably lie in French literature, down amongst the blackmailers and backstairs wire-pullers of Balzac's *La Comédie humaine*. Dickens, you feel, would have burlesqued Van Tromp into caricature. Stevenson has an instinctive understanding of the person he is, and the result – comic, self-engrossed and infinitely sinister – is a wonderfully convincing portrait.

– *D.J. Taylor, 2008*

The Story of a Lie

CHAPTER I
INTRODUCES THE ADMIRAL

When Dick Naseby was in Paris he made some odd acquaint-ances; for he was one of those who have ears to hear, and can use their eyes no less than their intelligence. He made as many thoughts as Stuart Mill; but his philosophy concerned flesh and blood, and was experimental as to its method. He was a type-hunter among mankind. He despised small game and insignificant personalities, whether in the shape of dukes or bagmen, letting them go by like seaweed; but show him a re-fined or powerful face, let him hear a plangent or a penetrating voice, fish for him with a living look in someone's eye, a passionate gesture, a meaning and ambiguous smile, and his mind was instantaneously awakened. 'There was a man, there was a woman,' he seemed to say, and he stood up to the task of comprehension with the delight of an artist in his art.

And indeed, rightly considered, this interest of his was an artistic interest. There is no science in the personal study of human nature. All comprehension is creation; the woman I love is somewhat of my handiwork; and the great lover, like the great painter, is he that can so embellish his subject as to make her more than human, whilst yet by a cunning art he has so based his apotheosis on the nature of the case that the woman can go on being a true woman, and give her character free play, and show littleness, or cherish spite, or be greedy of common pleasures, and he continue to worship without a thought of incongruity. To love a character is only the heroic way of understanding it. When we love, by some noble method of our own or some nobility of mien or nature in the other, we apprehend the loved one by what is noblest in ourselves. When we are merely studying an eccentricity, the

3

method of our study is but a series of allowances. To begin to understand is to begin to sympathise; for comprehension comes only when we have stated another's faults and virtues in terms of our own. Hence the proverbial toleration of artists for their own evil creations. Hence, too, it came about that Dick Naseby, a high-minded creature, and as scrupulous and brave a gentleman as you would want to meet, held in a sort of affection the various human creeping things whom he had met and studied.

One of these was Mr Peter Van Tromp, an English-speaking, two-legged animal of the international genus, and by profession of general and more than equivocal utility. Years before, he had been a painter of some standing in a colony, and portraits signed 'Van Tromp' had celebrated the greatness of colonial governors and judges. In those days he had been married, and driven his wife and infant daughter in a pony-trap. What were the steps of his declension? No one exactly knew. Here he was at least, and had been any time these past ten years, a sort of dismal parasite upon the foreigner in Paris.

It would be hazardous to specify his exact industry. Coarsely followed, it would have merited a name grown somewhat unfamiliar to our ears. Followed as he followed it, with a skilful reticence, in a kind of social chiaroscuro, it was still possible for the polite to call him a professional painter. His lair was in the Grand Hotel and the gaudiest cafés. There he might be seen jotting off a sketch with an air of some inspiration; and he was always affable, and one of the easiest of men to fall in talk withal. A conversation usually ripened into a peculiar sort of intimacy, and it was extraordinary how many little services Van Tromp contrived to render in the course of six-and-thirty hours. He occupied a position between a friend and a courier, which made him worse than embarrassing to repay. But those whom he obliged could always buy one of his villainous little pictures, or, where the favours had been prolonged and more than usually delicate, might order and pay for a large canvas, with perfect certainty that they would hear no more of the transaction.

Among resident artists he enjoyed celebrity of a non-professional sort. He had spent more money – no less than three individual fortunes, it was whispered – than any of his associates could ever hope to gain. Apart from his colonial career, he had been to Greece in a brigantine with four brass corronades; he had travelled Europe in a chaise and four, drawing bridle at the palace doors of German princes; queens of song and dance had followed him like sheep and paid his tailor's bills. And to behold him now, seeking small loans with plaintive condescension, sponging for breakfast on an art student of nineteen, a fallen Don Juan who had neglected to die at the propitious hour, had a colour of romance for young imaginations. His name and his bright past, seen through the prism of whispered gossip, had gained him the nickname of 'the Admiral'.

Dick found him one day at the receipt of custom, rapidly painting a pair of hens and a cock in a little watercolour sketching box, and now and then glancing at the ceiling like a man who should seek inspiration from the muse. Dick thought it remarkable that a painter should choose to work over an absinthe in a public café, and looked the man over. The aged rakishness of his appearance was set off by a youthful costume; he had disreputable grey hair and a disreputable sore, red nose; but the coat and the gesture, the outworks of the man, were still designed for show. Dick came up to his table and inquired if he might look at what the gentleman was doing. No one was so delighted as the Admiral.

'A bit of a thing,' said he. 'I just dash them off like that. I – I dash them off,' he added with a gesture.

'Quite so,' said Dick, who was appalled by the feebleness of the production.

'Understand me,' continued Van Tromp, 'I am a man of the world. And yet – once an artist always an artist. All of a sudden a thought takes me in the street; I become its prey: it's like a pretty woman; no use to struggle; I must – dash it off.'

'I see,' said Dick.

'Yes,' pursued the painter, 'it all comes easily, easily to me; it is not my business; it's a pleasure. Life is my business life – this great city, Paris – Paris after dark – its lights, its gardens, its odd corners. Aha!' he cried, 'to be young again! The heart is young, but the heels are leaden. A poor, mean business, to grow old! Nothing remains but the *coup d'oeil*, the contemplative man's enjoyment, Mr – ' and he paused for the name.

'Naseby,' returned Dick.

The other treated him at once to an exciting beverage, and expatiated on the pleasure of meeting a compatriot in a foreign land; to hear him, you would have thought they had encountered in Central Africa. Dick had never found any one take a fancy to him so readily, nor show it in an easier or less offensive manner. He seemed tickled with him as an elderly fellow about town might be tickled by a pleasant and witty lad; he indicated that he was no precisian, but in his wildest times had never been such a blade as he thought Dick. Dick protested, but in vain. This manner of carrying an intimacy at the bayonet's point was Van Tromp's stock-in-trade. With an older man he insinuated himself; with youth he imposed himself, and in the same breath imposed an ideal on his victim, who saw that he must work up to it or lose the esteem of this old and vicious patron. And what young man can bear to lose a character for vice?

At last, as it grew towards dinner time, 'Do you know Paris?' asked Van Tromp.

'Not so well as you, I am convinced,' said Dick.

'And so am I,' returned Van Tromp gaily. 'Paris! My young friend – you will allow me? – when you know Paris as I do, you will have seen Strange Things. I say no more; all I say is, Strange Things. We are men of the world, you and I, and in Paris, in the heart of civilised existence. This is an opportunity, Mr Naseby. Let us dine. Let me show you where to dine.'

Dick consented. On the way to dinner the Admiral showed him where to buy gloves, and made him buy them; where to buy cigars, and made him buy a vast store, some of which he obligingly accepted. At the restaurant he showed him what to order, with surprising consequences in the bill. What he made that night by his percentages it would be hard to estimate. And all the while Dick smilingly consented, understanding well that he was being done, but taking his losses in the pursuit of character as a hunter sacrifices his dogs. As for the Strange Things, the reader will be relieved to hear that they were no stranger than might have been expected, and he may find things quite as strange without the expense of a Van Tromp for guide. Yet he was a guide of no mean order, who made up for the poverty of what he had to show by a copious, imaginative commentary.

'And such,' said he, with a hiccup, 'such is Paris.'

'Pooh!' said Dick, who was tired of the performance.

The Admiral hung an ear, and looked up sidelong with a glimmer of suspicion.

'Good night,' said Dick, 'I'm tired.'

'So English!' cried Van Tromp, clutching him by the hand. 'So English! So blasé! Such a charming companion! Let me see you home.'

'Look here,' returned Dick, 'I have said good night, and now I'm going. You're an amusing old boy: I like you, in a sense; but here's an end of it for tonight. Not another cigar, not another grog, not another percentage out of me.'

'I beg your pardon!' cried the Admiral with dignity.

'Tut, man!' said Dick, 'you're not offended; you're a man of the world, I thought. I've been studying you, and it's over. Have I not paid for the lesson? *Au revoir*.'

Van Tromp laughed gaily, shook hands up to the elbows, hoped cordially they would meet again and that often, but looked after Dick as he departed with a tremor of indignation. After that they two not unfrequently fell in each other's way, and Dick would often treat the old boy to breakfast on a moderate scale and in a restaurant of his own selection. Often, too, he would lend Van Tromp the matter of a pound, in view of that gentleman's contemplated departure for Australia; there would be a scene of farewell almost touching in character, and a week or a month later they would meet on the same boulevard without surprise or embarrassment. And in the meantime Dick learned more about his acquaintance on all sides: heard of his yacht, his chaise and four, his brief season of celebrity amid a more confiding population, his daughter, of whom he loved to whimper in his cups, his sponging, parasitical, nameless way of life; and with each new detail something that was not merely interest nor yet altogether affection grew up in his mind towards this disreputable stepson of the arts. Ere he left Paris, Van Tromp was one of those whom he entertained to a farewell supper; and the old gentleman made the speech of the evening, and then fell below the table, weeping, smiling, paralysed.

CHAPTER II
A LETTER TO THE PAPERS

Old Mr Naseby had the sturdy, untutored nature of the upper middle class. The universe seemed plain to him. 'The thing's right,' he would say, or 'The thing's wrong'; and there was an end of it. There was a contained, prophetic energy in his utterances, even on the slightest affairs; he *saw* the damned thing; if you did not, it must be from perversity of will; and this sent the blood to his head. Apart from this, which made him an exacting companion, he was one of the most upright, hot-tempered, hot-headed old gentlemen in England. Florid, with white hair, the face of an old Jupiter, and the figure of an old foxhunter, he enlivened the vale of Thyme from end to end on his big, cantering chestnut.

He had a hearty respect for Dick as a lad of parts. Dick had a respect for his father as the best of men, tempered by the politic revolt of a youth who has to see to his own independence. Whenever the pair argued, they came to an open rupture; and arguments were frequent, for they were both positive, and both loved the work of the intelligence. It was a treat to hear Mr Naseby defending the Church of England in a volley of oaths, or supporting ascetic morals with an enthusiasm not entirely innocent of port wine. Dick used to wax indignant, and none the less so because, as his father was a skilful disputant, he found himself not seldom in the wrong. On these occasions, he would redouble in energy, and declare that black was white, and blue yellow, with much conviction and heat of manner; but in the morning such a licence of debate weighed upon him like a crime, and he would seek out his father, where he walked before breakfast on a terrace overlooking all the vale of Thyme.

'I have to apologise, sir, for last night –' he would begin.

'Of course you have,' the old gentleman would cut in cheerfully. 'You spoke like a fool. Say no more about it.'

'You do not understand me, sir. I refer to a particular point. I confess there is much force in your argument from the doctrine of possibilities.'

'Of course there is,' returned his father. 'Come down and look at the stables. Only,' he would add, 'bear this in mind, and do remember that a man of my age and experience knows more about what he is saying than a raw boy.'

He would utter the word 'boy' even more offensively than the average of fathers, and the light way in which he accepted these apologies cut Richard to the heart. The latter drew slighting comparisons, and remembered that he was the only one who ever apologised. This gave him a high station in his own esteem, and thus contributed indirectly to his better behaviour; for he was scrupulous as well as high-spirited, and prided himself on nothing more than on a just submission.

So things went on until the famous occasion when Mr Naseby, becoming engrossed in securing the election of a sound party candidate to Parliament, wrote a flaming letter to the papers. The letter had about every demerit of party letters in general; it was expressed with the energy of a believer; it was personal; it was a little more than half unfair, and about a quarter untrue. The old man did not mean to say what was untrue, you may be sure; but he had rashly picked up gossip, as his prejudice suggested, and now rashly launched it on the public with the sanction of his name.

'The Liberal candidate,' he concluded, 'is thus a public turncoat. Is that the sort of man we want? He has been given the lie, and has swallowed the insult. Is that the sort of man we want? I answer, No! With all the force of my conviction, I answer, *No!*'

And then he signed and dated the letter with an amateur's pride, and looked to be famous by the morrow.

Dick, who had heard nothing of the matter, was up first on that inauspicious day, and took the journal to an arbour in the garden. He found his father's manifesto in one column; and in another a leading article. 'No one that we are aware of,' ran the article, 'had consulted Mr Naseby on the subject, but if he had been appealed to by the whole body of electors, his letter would be none the less ungenerous and unjust to Mr Dalton. We do not choose to give the lie to Mr Naseby, for we are too well aware of the consequences; but we shall venture instead to print the facts of both cases referred to by this red-hot partisan in another portion of our issue. Mr Naseby is of course a large proprietor in our neighbourhood; but fidelity to facts, decent feeling, and English grammar, are all of them qualities more important than the possession of land. Mr — is doubtless a great man; in his large gardens and that half mile of greenhouses, where he has probably ripened his intellect and temper, he may say what he will to his hired vassals, but (as the Scotch say):

here
He mauna think to domineer.

'Liberalism,' continued the anonymous journalist, 'is of too free and sound a growth,' etc.

Richard Naseby read the whole thing from beginning to end; and a crushing shame fell upon his spirit. His father had played the fool; he had gone out noisily to war, and come back with confusion. The moment that his trumpets sounded, he had been disgracefully unhorsed. There was no question as to the facts; they were one and all against the Squire. Richard would have given his ears to have suppressed the issue; but as that could not be done, he had his horse saddled, and, furnishing himself with a convenient staff, rode off at once to Thymebury.

The editor was at breakfast in a large, sad apartment. The absence of furniture, the extreme meanness of the meal, and the haggard, bright-eyed, consumptive look of the culprit, unmanned our hero; but he clung to his stick, and was stout and warlike.

'You wrote the article in this morning's paper?' he demanded.

'You are young Mr Naseby? I *published* it,' replied the editor, rising.

'My father is an old man,' said Richard; and then with an outburst, 'And a damned sight finer fellow than either you or Dalton!' He stopped and swallowed; he was determined that all should go with regularity. 'I have but one question to put to you, sir,' he resumed. 'Granted that my father was misinformed, would it not have been more decent to withhold the letter and communicate with him in private?'

'Believe me,' returned the editor, 'that alternative was not open to me. Mr Naseby told me in a note that he had sent his letter to three other journals, and in fact threatened me with what he called exposure if I kept it back from mine. I am really concerned at what has happened; I sympathise and approve of your emotion, young gentleman; but the attack on Mr Dalton was gross, very gross, and I had no choice but to offer him my columns to reply. Party has its duties, sir,' added the scribe, kindling, as one who should propose a sentiment, 'and the attack was gross.'

Richard stood for half a minute digesting the answer; and then the god of fair play came uppermost in his heart, and murmuring 'Good morning,' he made his escape into the street.

His horse was not hurried on the way home, and he was late for breakfast. The Squire was standing with his back to the fire in a state bordering on apoplexy, his fingers violently knitted under his coat tails. As Richard came in, he opened and shut his mouth like a codfish, and his eyes protruded.

'Have you seen that, sir?' he cried, nodding towards the paper.

'Yes, sir,' said Richard.

'Oh, you've read it, have you?'

'Yes, I have read it,' replied Richard, looking at his foot.

'Well,' demanded the old gentleman, 'and what have you to say to it, sir?'

'You seem to have been misinformed,' said Dick.

'Well? What then? Is your mind so sterile, sir? Have you not a word of comment? no proposal?'

'I fear, sir, you must apologise to Mr Dalton. It would be more handsome, indeed it would be only just, and a free acknowledgment would go far –' Richard paused, no language appearing delicate enough to suit the case.

'That is a suggestion which should have come from me, sir,' roared the father. 'It is out of place upon your lips. It is not the thought of a loyal son. Why, sir, if my father had been plunged in such deplorable circumstances, I should have thrashed the editor of that vile sheet within an inch of his life. I should have thrashed the man, sir. It would have been the action of an ass; but it would have shown that I had the blood and the natural affections of a man. Son? You are no son, no son of mine, sir!'

'Sir!' said Dick.

'I'll tell you what you are, sir,' pursued the Squire. 'You're a Benthamite. I disown you. Your mother would have died for shame; there was no modern cant about your mother; she thought – she said to me, sir – I'm glad she's in her grave, Dick Naseby. Misinformed! Misinformed, sir? Have you no loyalty, no spring, no natural affections? Are you clockwork, hey? Away! This is no place for you. Away!' (waving his hands in the air). 'Go away! Leave me!'

At this moment Dick beat a retreat in a disarray of nerves, a whistling and clamour of his own arteries, and in short in such a final bodily disorder as made him alike incapable of speech or hearing. And in the midst of all this turmoil a sense of unpardonable injustice remained graven in his memory.

CHAPTER III
IN THE ADMIRAL'S NAME

There was no return to the subject. Dick and his father were henceforth on terms of coldness. The upright old gentleman grew more upright when he met his son, buckrammed with immortal anger; he asked after Dick's health, and discussed the weather and the crops with an appalling courtesy; his pronunciation was *point-device*, his voice was distant, distinct, and sometimes almost trembling with suppressed indignation.

As for Dick, it seemed to him as if his life had come abruptly to an end. He came out of his theories and clevernesses; his premature man-of-the-worldness, on which he had prided himself on his travels, 'shrank like a thing ashamed' before this real sorrow. Pride, wounded honour, pity and respect tussled together daily in his heart; and now he was within an ace of throwing himself upon his father's mercy, and now of slipping forth at night and coming back no more to Naseby House. He suffered from the sight of his father, nay, even from the neighbourhood of this familiar valley, where every corner had its legend, and he was besieged with memories of childhood. If he fled into a new land, and among none but strangers, he might escape his destiny, who knew? and begin again light-heartedly. From that chief peak of the hills, that now and then, like an uplifted finger, shone in an arrow of sunlight through the broken clouds, the shepherd in clear weather might perceive the shining of the sea. There, he thought, was hope. But his heart failed him when he saw the Squire; and he remained. His fate was not that of the voyager by sea and land; he was to travel in the spirit, and begin his journey sooner than he supposed.

For it chanced one day that his walk led him into a portion of the uplands which was almost unknown to him. Scrambling through some rough woods, he came out upon a moorland reaching towards the hills. A few lofty Scotch firs grew hard by upon a knoll; a clear fountain near the foot of the knoll sent up a miniature streamlet which meandered in the heather. A shower had just skimmed by, but now the sun shone brightly, and the air smelt of the pines and the grass. On a stone under the trees sat a young lady sketching. We have learned to think of women in a sort of symbolic transfiguration, based on clothes; and one of the readiest ways in which we conceive our mistress is as a composite thing, principally petticoats. But humanity has triumphed over clothes; the look, the touch of a dress has become alive; and the woman who stitched herself into these material integuments has now permeated right through and gone out to the tip of her skirt. It was only a black dress that caught Dick Naseby's eye; but it took possession of his mind, and all other thoughts departed. He drew near, and the girl turned round. Her face startled him; it was a face he wanted; and he took it in at once like breathing air.

'I beg your pardon,' he said, taking off his hat, 'you are sketching.'

'Oh!' she exclaimed, 'for my own amusement. I despise the thing.'

'Ten to one, you do yourself injustice,' returned Dick. 'Besides, it's a freemasonry. I sketch myself, and you know what that implies.'

'No. What?' she asked.

'Two things,' he answered. 'First, that I am no very difficult critic; and second, that I have a right to see your picture.'

She covered the block with both her hands. 'Oh no,' she said; 'I am ashamed.'

'Indeed, I might give you a hint,' said Dick. 'Although no artist myself, I have known many; in Paris I had many for friends, and used to prowl among studios.'

'In Paris?' she cried, with a leap of light into her eyes. 'Did you ever meet Mr Van Tromp?'

'I? Yes. Why, you're not the Admiral's daughter, are you?'

'The Admiral? Do they call him that?' she cried. 'Oh, how nice, how nice of them! It is the younger men who call him so, is it not?'

'Yes,' said Dick, somewhat heavily.

'You can understand now,' she said, with an unspeakable accent of contented noble-minded pride, 'why it is I do not choose to show my sketch. Van Tromp's daughter! The Admiral's daughter! I delight in that name. The Admiral! And so you know my father?'

'Well,' said Dick, 'I met him often; we were even intimate. He may have mentioned my name – Naseby.'

'He writes so little. He is so busy, so devoted to his art! I have had a half wish,' she added, laughing, 'that my father was a plainer man, whom I could help – to whom I could be a credit; but only sometimes, you know, and with only half my heart. For a great painter! You have seen his works?'

'I have seen some of them,' returned Dick, 'they – they are very nice.'

She laughed aloud. 'Nice?' she repeated. 'I see you don't care much for art.'

'Not much,' he admitted, 'but I know that many people are glad to buy Mr Van Tromp's pictures.'

'Call him the Admiral!' she cried. 'It sounds kindly and familiar; and I like to think that he is appreciated and looked up to by young painters. He has not always been appreciated; he had a cruel life for many years; and when I think' – there were tears in her eyes – 'when I think of that, I feel inclined to be a fool,' she broke off. 'And now I shall go home. You have filled me full of happiness; for think, Mr Naseby, I have not seen my father since I was six years old; and yet he is in my thoughts all day! You must come and call on me; my aunt will be delighted, I am sure; and then you will tell me all – all about my father, will you not?'

Dick helped her to get her sketching traps together, and when all was ready, she gave Dick her hand and a frank return of pressure.

'You are my father's friend,' she said, 'we shall be great friends too. You must come and see me soon.'

Then she was gone down the hillside at a run, and Dick stood by himself in a state of some bewilderment and even distress. There were elements of laughter in the business, but the black dress, and the face that belonged to it, and the hand that he had held in his, inclined him to a serious view. What was he, under the circumstances, called upon to do? Perhaps to avoid the girl? Well, he would think about that. Perhaps to break the truth to her? Why, ten to one, such was her infatuation, he would fail. Perhaps to keep up the illusion, to colour the raw facts, to help her to false ideas, while yet not plainly stating falsehoods? Well, he would see about that; he would also see about avoiding the girl. He saw about this last so well, that the next afternoon beheld him on his way to visit her.

In the meantime the girl had gone straight home, light as a bird, tremulous with joy, to the little cottage where she lived alone with a maiden aunt; and to that lady, a grim, sixty-years-old Scotchwoman, with a nodding head, communicated news of her encounter and invitation.

'A friend of his?' cried the aunt. 'What like is he? What did ye say was his name?'

She was dead silent, and stared at the old woman, darkling. Then, very slowly, 'I said he was my father's friend; I have invited him to my house, and come he shall,' she said; and with that she walked off to her room, where she sat staring at the wall all the evening. Miss M'Glashan, for that was the aunt's name, read a large Bible in the kitchen with some of the joys of martyrdom.

It was perhaps half past three when Dick presented himself, rather scrupulously dressed, before the cottage door; he knocked, and a voice bade him enter. The kitchen, which opened directly off the garden, was somewhat darkened by foliage; but he could see her as she approached from the far end to meet him. The second sight of her surprised him. Her strong black brows spoke of temper easily aroused and hard to quiet; her mouth was small, nervous and weak; there was something dangerous and sulky underlying, in her nature, much that was honest, compassionate, and even noble.

'My father's name,' she said, 'has made you very welcome.'

And she gave him her hand, with a sort of curtsy. It was a pretty greeting, although somewhat mannered; and Dick felt himself among the gods. She led him through the kitchen to a parlour, and presented him to Miss M'Glashan.

'Esther,' said the aunt, 'see and make Mr Naseby his tea.'

And as soon as the girl was gone upon this hospitable intent, the old woman crossed the room and came quite near to Dick as if in menace.

'Ye know that man?' she asked in an imperious whisper.

'Mr Van Tromp?' said Dick. 'Yes, I know him.'

'Well, and what brings ye here?' she said. 'I couldn't save the mother – her that's dead – but the bairn!' She had a note in her voice that filled poor Dick with consternation. 'Man,' she went on, 'what is it now? Is it money?'

'My dear lady,' said Dick, 'I think you misinterpret my position. I am young Mr Naseby of Naseby House. My acquaintance with Mr Van Tromp is really very slender; I am only afraid that Miss Van Tromp has exaggerated our intimacy in her own imagination. I know positively nothing of his private affairs, and do not care to know. I met him casually in Paris – that is all.'

Miss M'Glashan drew a long breath. 'In Paris?' she said. 'Well, and what do you think of him? – what do ye think of him?' she repeated, with a different scansion, as Richard, who had not much taste for such a question, kept her waiting for an answer.

'I found him a very agreeable companion,' he said.

'Ay,' said she, 'did ye! And how does he win his bread?'

'I fancy,' he gasped, 'that Mr Van Tromp has many generous friends.'

'I'll warrant!' she sneered; and before Dick could find more to say, she was gone from the room.

Esther returned with the tea things, and sat down.

'Now,' she said cosily, 'tell me all about my father.'

'He,' stammered Dick, 'he is a very agreeable companion.'

'I shall begin to think it is more than you are, Mr Naseby,' she said, with a laugh. 'I am his daughter, you forget. Begin at the beginning, and tell me all you have seen of him, all he said and all you answered. You must have met somewhere; begin with that.'

So with that he began: how he had found the Admiral painting in a cafe; how his art so possessed him that he could not wait till he got home to – well, to dash off his idea; how (this in reply to a question) his idea consisted of a cock crowing and two hens eating corn; how he was fond of cocks and hens; how this did not lead him to neglect more ambitious forms of art; how he had a picture in his studio of a Greek subject which was said to be remarkable from several points of view; how no one had seen it nor knew the precise site of the studio in which it was being vigorously though secretly confected; how (in answer to a suggestion) this shyness was common to the Admiral, Michelangelo, and others; how they (Dick and Van Tromp) had struck up an acquaintance at once, and dined together that same night; how he (the Admiral) had once given money to a beggar; how he spoke with effusion of his little daughter; how he had once borrowed money to send her a doll – a trait worthy of Newton, she being then in her nineteenth year at least; how, if the doll never arrived (which it appeared it never did), the trait was only more characteristic of the highest order of creative intellect; how he was – no, not beautiful – striking, yes, Dick would go so far, decidedly striking in appearance; how his boots were made to lace and his coat was black, not cut-away, a frock; and so on, and so on by the yard. It was astonishing how few lies were necessary. After all, people exaggerated the difficulty of life. A little steering, just a touch of the rudder now and then, and with a willing listener there is no limit to the domain of equivocal speech. Sometimes Miss M'Glashan made a freezing sojourn in the parlour, and then the task seemed unaccountably more difficult; but to Esther, who was all eyes and ears, her face alight with interest, his stream of language flowed without break or stumble, and his mind was ever fertile in ingenious evasions and –

What an afternoon it was for Esther!

'Ah!' she said at last, 'it's good to hear all this! My aunt, you should know, is narrow and too religious; she cannot understand an artist's life. It does not frighten me,' she added grandly, 'I am an artist's daughter.'

With that speech, Dick consoled himself for his imposture; she was not deceived so grossly after all; and then if a fraud, was not the fraud piety itself? – and what could be more obligatory than to keep alive in the heart of a daughter that filial trust and honour which, even although misplaced, became her like a jewel of the mind? There might be another thought, a shade of cowardice, a selfish desire to please; poor Dick was merely human, and what would you have had him do?

CHAPTER IV
ESTHER ON THE FILIAL RELATION

A month later Dick and Esther met at the stile beside the crossroads; had there been anyone to see them but the birds and summer insects, it would have been remarked that they met after a different fashion from the day before. Dick took her in his arms, and their lips were set together for a long while. Then he held her at arm's length, and they looked straight into each other's eyes.

'Esther!' he said; you should have heard his voice!

'Dick!' said she.

'My darling!'

It was some time before they started for their walk; he kept an arm about her, and their sides were close together as they walked; the sun, the birds, the west wind running among the trees, a pressure, a look, the grasp tightening round a single finger, these things stood them in lieu of thought and filled their hearts with joy. The path they were following led them through a wood of pine trees carpeted with heather and blueberry, and upon this pleasant carpet, Dick, not without some seriousness, made her sit down.

'Esther!' he began, 'there is something you ought to know. You know my father is a rich man, and you would think, now that we love each other, we might marry when we pleased. But I fear, darling, we may have long to wait, and shall want all our courage.'

'I have courage for anything,' she said, 'I have all I want; with you and my father, I am so well off, and waiting is made so happy, that I could wait a lifetime and not weary.'

He had a sharp pang at the mention of the Admiral. 'Hear me out,' he continued. 'I ought to have told you this before;

but it is a thought I shrink from; if it were possible, I should not tell you even now. My poor father and I are scarce on speaking terms.'

'Your father,' she repeated, turning pale.

'It must sound strange to you, but yet I cannot think I am to blame,' he said. 'I will tell you how it happened.'

'Oh Dick!' she said, when she had heard him to an end, 'how brave you are, and how proud. Yet I would not be proud with a father. I would tell him all.'

'What!' cried Dick, 'go in months after, and brag that I had meant to thrash the man, and then didn't. And why? Because my father had made a bigger ass of himself than I supposed. My dear, that's nonsense.'

She winced at his words and drew away. 'But when that is all he asks,' she pleaded. 'If he only knew that you had felt that impulse, it would make him so proud and happy. He would see you were his own son after all, and had the same thoughts and the same chivalry of spirit. And then you did yourself injustice when you spoke just now. It was because the editor was weak and poor and excused himself, that you repented your first determination. Had he been a big red man, with whiskers, you would have beaten him – you know you would – if Mr Naseby had been ten times more committed. Do you think, if you can tell it to me, and I understand at once, that it would be more difficult to tell it to your own father, or that he would not be more ready to sympathise with you than I am? And I love you, Dick; but then he is your father.'

'My dear,' said Dick, desperately, 'you do not understand; you do not know what it is to be treated with daily want of comprehension and daily small injustices, through childhood and boyhood and manhood, until you despair of a hearing, until the thing rides you like a nightmare, until you almost hate the sight of the man you love, and who's your father after all. In short, Esther, you don't know what it is to have a father, and that's what blinds you.'

'I see,' she said musingly, 'you mean that I am fortunate in my father. But I am not so fortunate after all; you forget, I do not know him; it is you who know him; he is already more your father than mine.' And here she took his hand. Dick's heart had grown as cold as ice. 'But I am sorry for you, too,' she continued, 'it must be very sad and lonely.'

'You misunderstand me,' said Dick, chokingly. 'My father is the best man I know in all this world; he is worth a hundred of me, only he doesn't understand me, and he can't be made to.'

There was a silence for a while. 'Dick,' she began again, 'I am going to ask a favour, it's the first since you said you loved me. May I see your father – see him pass, I mean, where he will not observe me?'

'Why?' asked Dick.

'It is a fancy; you forget, I am romantic about fathers.'

The hint was enough for Dick; he consented with haste, and full of hang-dog penitence and disgust, took her down by a backway and planted her in the shrubbery, whence she might see the Squire ride by to dinner. There they both sat silent, but holding hands, for nearly half an hour. At last the trotting of a horse sounded in the distance, the park gates opened with a clang, and then Mr Naseby appeared, with stooping shoulders and a heavy, bilious countenance, languidly rising to the trot. Esther recognised him at once; she had often seen him before, though with her huge indifference for all that lay outside the circle of her love, she had never so much as wondered who he was; but now she recognised him, and found him ten years older, leaden and springless, and stamped by an abiding sorrow.

'Oh Dick, Dick!' she said, and the tears began to shine upon her face as she hid it in his bosom; his own fell thickly too. They had a sad walk home, and that night, full of love and good counsel, Dick exerted every art to please his father, to convince him of his respect and affection, to heal up this breach of kindness, and reunite two hearts. But alas! the Squire was sick and peevish; he had been all day glooming over Dick's estrangement – for so he put it to himself – and now with growls, cold words, and the cold shoulder, he beat off all advances, and entrenched himself in a just resentment.

CHAPTER V
THE PRODIGAL FATHER MAKES
HIS DEBUT AT HOME

That took place upon a Tuesday. On the Thursday following, as Dick was walking by appointment, earlier than usual,
in the direction of the cottage, he was appalled to meet in
the lane a fly from Thymebury, containing the human form
of Miss M'Glashan. The lady did not deign to remark him
in her passage; her face was suffused with tears, and expressed much concern for the packages by which she was
surrounded. He stood still, and asked himself what this
circumstance might portend. It was so beautiful a day that
he was loath to forecast evil, yet something must perforce
have happened at the cottage, and that of a decisive nature;
for here was Miss M'Glashan on her travels, with a small
patrimony in brown paper parcels, and the old lady's bearing
implied hot battle and unqualified defeat. Was the house to
be closed against him? Was Esther left alone, or had some
new protector made his appearance from among the millions
of Europe? It is the character of love to loathe the near
relatives of the loved one; chapters in the history of the
human race have justified this feeling, and the conduct of
uncles, in particular, has frequently met with censure from
the independent novelist. Miss M'Glashan was now seen in
the rosy colours of regret; whoever succeeded her, Dick felt
the change would be for the worse. He hurried forward in
this spirit; his anxiety grew upon him with every step; as he
entered the garden a voice fell upon his ear, and he was once
more arrested, not this time by doubt, but by indubitable
certainty of ill.

The thunderbolt had fallen; the Admiral was here.

Dick would have retreated, in the panic terror of the moment; but Esther kept a bright lookout when her lover was expected. In a twinkling she was by his side, brimful of news and pleasure, too glad to notice his embarrassment, and in one of those golden transports of exultation which transcend not only words but caresses. She took him by the end of the fingers (reaching forward to take them, for her great preoccupation was to save time), she drew him towards her, pushed him past her in the door, and planted him face to face with Mr Van Tromp, in a suit of French country velveteens and with a remarkable carbuncle on his nose. Then, as though this was the end of what she could endure in the way of joy, Esther turned and ran out of the room.

The two men remained looking at each other with some confusion on both sides. Van Tromp was naturally the first to recover; he put out his hand with a fine gesture.

'And you know my little lass, my Esther?' he said. 'This is pleasant; this is what I have conceived of home. A strange word for the old rover; but we all have a taste for home and the home-like, disguise it how we may. It has brought me here, Mr Naseby,' he concluded, with an intonation that would have made his fortune on the stage, so just, so sad, so dignified, so like a man of the world and a philosopher, 'and you see a man who is content.'

'I see,' said Dick.

'Sit down,' continued the parasite, setting the example. 'Fortune has gone against me. (I am just sirrupping a little brandy – after my journey.) I was going down, Mr Naseby; between you and me, I was *décavé*; I borrowed fifty francs, smuggled my valise past the concierge – a work of considerable tact – and here I am!'

'Yes,' said Dick, 'and here you are.' He was quite idiotic.

Esther, at this moment, re-entered the room.

'Are you glad to see him?' she whispered in his ear, the pleasure in her voice almost bursting through the whisper into song.

'Oh yes,' said Dick, 'very.'

'I knew you would be,' she replied, 'I told him how you loved him.'

'Help yourself,' said the Admiral, 'help yourself; and let us drink to a new existence.'

'To a new existence,' repeated Dick; and he raised the tumbler to his lips, but set it down untasted. He had had enough of novelties for one day.

Esther was sitting on a stool beside her father's feet, holding her knees in her arms, and looking with pride from one to the other of her two visitors. Her eyes were so bright that you were never sure if there were tears in them or not; little voluptuous shivers ran about her body; sometimes she nestled her chin into her throat, sometimes threw back her head, with ecstasy; in a word, she was in that state when it is said of people that they cannot contain themselves for happiness. It would be hard to exaggerate the agony of Richard.

And, in the meantime, Van Tromp ran on interminably.

'I never forget a friend,' said he, 'nor yet an enemy: of the latter, I never had but two – myself and the public; and I fancy I have had my vengeance pretty freely out of both.' He chuckled. 'But those days are done. Van Tromp is no more. He was a man who had successes; I believe you knew I had successes – to which we shall refer no further,' pulling down his neckcloth with a smile. 'That man exists no more: by an exercise of will I have destroyed him. There is something like it in the poets. First, a brilliant and conspicuous career – the observed, I may say, of all observers, including the bum-bailie:

and then, presto! a quiet, sly, old, rustic *bonhomme*, cultivating roses. In Paris, Mr Naseby – '

'Call him Richard, father,' said Esther.

'Richard, if he will allow me. Indeed, we are old friends, and now near neighbours; and, *à propos*, how are we off for neighbours, Richard? The cottage stands, I think, upon your father's land – a family which I respect – and the wood, I understand, is Lord Trevanion's. Not that I care; I am an old Bohemian. I have cut society with a cut direct; I cut it when I was prosperous, and now I reap my reward, and can cut it with dignity in my declension. These are our little *amours propres*, my daughter: your father must respect himself. Thank you, yes; just a leetle, leetle, tiny – thanks, thanks; you spoil me. But, as I was saying, Richard, or was about to say, my daughter has been allowed to rust; her aunt was a mere duenna; hence, in parenthesis, Richard, her distrust of me; my nature and that of the duenna are poles asunder – poles! But, now that I am here, now that I have given up the fight, and live henceforth for one only of my works – I have the modesty to say it is my best – my daughter – well, we shall put all that to rights. The neighbours, Richard?'

Dick was understood to say that there were many good families in the Vale of Thyme.

'You shall introduce us,' said the Admiral.

Dick's shirt was wet; he made a lumbering excuse to go; which Esther explained to herself by a fear of intrusion, and so set down to the merit side of Dick's account, while she proceeded to detain him.

'Before our walk?' she cried. 'Never! I must have my walk.'

'Let us all go,' said the Admiral, rising.

'You do not know that you are wanted,' she cried, leaning on his shoulder with a caress. 'I might wish to speak to my old friend about my new father. But you shall come today, you shall do all you want; I have set my heart on spoiling you.'

'I will just take *one* drop more,' said the Admiral, stooping to help himself to brandy. 'It is surprising how this journey has fatigued me. But I am growing old, I am growing old, I am growing old, and – I regret to add – bald.'

He cocked a white wide-awake coquettishly upon his head – the habit of the ladykiller clung to him; and Esther had already thrown on her hat, and was ready, while he was still studying the result in a mirror: the carbuncle had somewhat painfully arrested his attention.

'We are papa now, we must be respectable,' he said to Dick, in explanation of his dandyism: and then he went to a bundle and chose himself a staff. Where were the elegant canes of his Parisian epoch? This was a support for age, and designed for rustic scenes. Dick began to see and appreciate the man's enjoyment in a new part, when he saw how carefully he had 'made it up'. He had invented a gait for this first country stroll with his daughter, which was admirably in key. He walked with fatigue, he leaned upon the staff, he looked round him with a sad, smiling sympathy on all that he beheld; he even asked the name of a plant, and rallied himself gently for an old town bird, ignorant of nature. 'This country life will make me young again,' he sighed. They reached the top of the hill towards the first hour of evening; the sun was descending heaven, the colour had all drawn into the west; the hills were modelled in their least contour by the soft, slanting shine; and the wide moorlands, veined with glens and hazelwoods, ran west and north in a hazy glory of light. Then the painter wakened in Van Tromp.

'Gad, Dick,' he cried, 'what value!'

An ode in four hundred lines would not have seemed so touching to Esther; her eyes filled with happy tears; yes, here

31

was the father of whom she had dreamed, whom Dick had described; simple, enthusiastic, unworldly, kind, a painter at heart, and a fine gentleman in manner.

And just then the Admiral perceived a house by the wayside, and something depending over the house door which might be construed as a sign by the hopeful and thirsty.

'Is that,' he asked, pointing with his stick, 'an inn?'

There was a marked change in his voice, as though he attached importance to the inquiry: Esther listened, hoping she should hear wit or wisdom.

Dick said it was.

'You know it?' inquired the Admiral.

'I have passed it a hundred times, but that is all,' replied Dick.

'Ah,' said Van Tromp, with a smile, and shaking his head, 'you are not an old campaigner; you have the world to learn. Now I, you see, find an inn so very near my own home, and my first thought is – my neighbours. I shall go forward and make my neighbours' acquaintance; no, you needn't come; I shall not be a moment.'

And he walked off briskly towards the inn, leaving Dick alone with Esther on the road.

'Dick,' she exclaimed, 'I am so glad to get a word with you; I am so happy, I have such a thousand things to say; and I want you to do me a favour. Imagine, he has come without a paint-box, without an easel; and I want him to have all. I want you to get them for me in Thymebury. You saw, this moment, how his heart turned to painting. They can't live without it,' she added; meaning perhaps Van Tromp and Michelangelo.

Up to that moment, she had observed nothing amiss in Dick's behaviour. She was too happy to be curious; and his silence, in presence of the great and good being whom she called her father, had seemed both natural and praiseworthy. But, now that they were alone, she became conscious of a barrier between her lover and herself, and alarm sprang up in her heart.

'Dick,' she cried, 'you don't love me.'

'I do that,' he said heartily.

'But you are unhappy; you are strange; you – you are not glad to see my father,' she concluded, with a break in her voice.

'Esther,' he said, 'I tell you that I love you; if you love me, you know what that means, and that all I wish is to see you happy. Do you think I cannot enjoy your pleasures? Esther, I do. If I am uneasy, if I am alarmed, if – oh, believe me, try and believe in me,' he cried, giving up argument with perhaps a happy inspiration.

But the girl's suspicions were aroused; and, though she pressed the matter no further (indeed, her father was already seen returning), it by no means left her thoughts. At one moment she simply resented the selfishness of a man who had obtruded his dark looks and passionate language on her joy; for there is nothing that a woman can less easily forgive than the language of a passion which, even if only for the moment, she does not share. At another, she suspected him of jealousy against her father; and for that, although she could see excuses for it, she yet despised him. And at least, in one way or the other, here was the dangerous beginning of a separation between two hearts. Esther found herself at variance with her sweetest friend; she could no longer look into his heart and find it written with the same language as her own; she could no longer think of him as the sun which radiated happiness upon her life, for she had turned to him once, and he had breathed upon her black and chilly, radiated blackness and frost. To put the whole matter in a word, she was beginning, although ever so slightly, to fall out of love.

CHAPTER VI
THE PRODIGAL FATHER GOES ON
FROM STRENGTH TO STRENGTH

We will not follow all the steps of the Admiral's return and installation, but hurry forward towards the catastrophe, merely chronicling by the way a few salient incidents, wherein we must rely entirely upon the evidence of Richard, for Esther to this day has never opened her mouth upon this trying passage of her life, and as for the Admiral – well, that naval officer, although still alive, and now more suitably installed in a seaport town where he has a telescope and a flag in his front garden, is incapable of throwing the slightest gleam of light upon the affair. Often and often has he remarked to the present writer, 'If I know what it was all about, sir, I'll be – ' in short, be what I hope he will not. And then he will look across at his daughter's portrait, a photograph, shake his head with an amused appearance, and mix himself another grog by way of consolation. Once I heard him go farther, and express his feelings with regard to Esther in a single but eloquent word. 'A minx, sir,' he said, not in anger, rather in amusement: and he cordially drank her health upon the back of it. His worst enemy must admit him to be a man without malice; he never bore a grudge in his life, lacking the necessary taste and industry of attention.

Yet it was during this obscure period that the drama was really performed; and its scene was in the heart of Esther, shut away from all eyes. Had this warm, upright, sullen girl been differently used by destiny, had events come upon her even in a different succession, for some things lead easily to others, the whole course of this tale would have been changed, and Esther never would have run away. As it was, through a series of acts

35

and words of which we know but few, and a series of thoughts which anyone may imagine for himself, she was awakened in four days from the dream of a life.

The first tangible cause of disenchantment was when Dick brought home a painter's arsenal on Friday evening. The Admiral was in the chimney-corner, once more 'sirrupping' some brandy and water, and Esther sat at the table at work. They both came forward to greet the new arrival; and the girl, relieving him of his monstrous burthen, proceeded to display her offerings to her father. Van Tromp's countenance fell several degrees; he became quite querulous.

'God bless me,' he said; and then, 'I must really ask you not to interfere, child,' in a tone of undisguised hostility.

'Father,' she said, 'forgive me; I knew you had given up your art – '

'Oh yes!' cried the Admiral; 'I've done with it to the Judgement Day!'

'Pardon me again,' she said firmly, 'but I do not, I cannot think that you are right in this. Suppose the world is unjust, suppose that no one understands you, you have still a duty to yourself. And, oh, don't spoil the pleasure of your coming home to me; show me that you can be my father and yet not neglect your destiny. I am not like some daughters; I will not be jealous of your art, and I will try to understand it.'

The situation was odiously farcical. Richard groaned under it; he longed to leap forward and denounce the humbug. And the humbug himself? Do you fancy he was easier in his mind? I am sure, on the other hand, that he was acutely miserable; and he betrayed his sufferings by a perfectly silly and un-dignified access of temper, during which he broke his pipe in several pieces, threw his brandy and water in the fire, and employed words which were very plain, although the drift of them was somewhat vague. It was of very brief duration. Van Tromp was himself again, and in a most delightful humour within three minutes of the first explosion.

'I am an old fool,' he said frankly. 'I was spoiled when a child. As for you, Esther, you take after your mother; you have a morbid sense of duty, particularly for others; strive against it, my dear – strive against it. And as for the pigments, well, I'll use them, some of these days; and, to show that I'm in earnest, I'll get Dick here to prepare a canvas.'

Dick was put to this menial task forthwith, the Admiral not even watching how he did, but quite occupied with another grog and a pleasant vein of talk.

A little after Esther arose, and making some pretext, good or bad, went off to bed. Dick was left hobbled by the canvas, and was subjected to Van Tromp for about an hour.

The next day, Saturday, it is believed that little intercourse took place between Esther and her father; but towards the afternoon Dick met the latter returning from the direction of the inn, where he had struck up quite a friendship with the landlord. Dick wondered who paid for these excursions, and at the thought that the reprobate must get his pocket money where he got his board and lodging, from poor Esther's generosity, he had it almost in his heart to knock the old gentleman down. He, on his part, was full of airs and graces and geniality.

'Dear Dick,' he said, taking his arm, 'this is neighbourly of you; it shows your tact to meet me when I had a wish for you. I am in pleasant spirits; and it is then that I desire a friend.'

'I am glad to hear you are so happy,' retorted Dick bitterly. 'There's certainly not much to trouble *you*.'

'No,' assented the Admiral, 'not much. I got out of it in time; and here – well, here everything pleases me. I am plain in my tastes. '*A propos*, you have never asked me how I liked my daughter?'

'No,' said Dick roundly; 'I certainly have not.'

'Meaning you will not. And why, Dick? She is my daughter, of course; but then I am a man of the world and a man of taste, and perfectly qualified to give an opinion with impartiality – yes, Dick, with impartiality. Frankly, I am not disappointed in her. She has good looks; she has them from her mother. So I may say I *chose* her looks. She is devoted, quite devoted to me – '

'She is the best woman in the world!' broke out Dick.

'Dick,' cried the Admiral, stopping short; 'I have been expecting this. Let us – let us go back to the Trevanion Arms and talk this matter out over a bottle.'

'Certainly not,' went on Dick. 'You have had far too much already.'

The parasite was on the point of resenting this; but a look at Dick's face, and some recollection of the terms on which they had stood in Paris, came to the aid of his wisdom and restrained him.

'As you please,' he said, 'although I don't know what you mean – nor care. But let us walk, if you prefer it. You are still a young man; when you are my age – but, however, to continue. You please me, Dick; you have pleased me from the first; and to say truth, Esther is a trifle fantastic, and will be better when she is married. She has means of her own, as of course you are aware. They come, like the looks, from her poor, dear, good creature of a mother. She was blessed in her mother. I mean she shall be blessed in her husband, and you are the man, Dick, you and not another. This very night I will sound her affections.'

Dick stood aghast.

'Mr Van Tromp, I implore you,' he said, 'do what you please with yourself, but, for God's sake, let your daughter alone.'

'It is my duty,' replied the Admiral, 'and between ourselves, you rogue, my inclination too. I am as matchmaking as a dowager. It will be more discreet for you to stay away tonight. Farewell. You leave your case in good hands; I have the tact of these little matters by heart; it is not my first attempt.'

All arguments were in vain; the old rascal stuck to his point; nor did Richard conceal from himself how seriously this might injure his prospects, and he fought hard. Once there came a glimmer of hope. The Admiral again proposed an adjournment to the Trevanion Arms, and when Dick had once more refused, it hung for a moment in the balance whether or not the old toper would return there by himself. Had he done so, of course Dick could have taken to his heels, and warned Esther of what was coming, and of how it had begun. But the Admiral, after a pause, decided for the brandy at home, and made off in that direction.

We have no details of the sounding.

Next day the Admiral was observed in the parish church, very properly dressed. He found the places, and joined in response and hymn, as to the manner born; and his appearance, as he intended it should, attracted some attention among the worshippers. Old Naseby, for instance, had observed him.

'There was a drunken-looking blackguard opposite us in church,' he said to his son as they drove home, 'do you know who he was?'

'Some fellow à Van Tromp, I believe,' said Dick.

'A foreigner, too!' observed the Squire.

Dick could not sufficiently congratulate himself on the escape he had effected. Had the Admiral met him with his father, what would have been the result? And could such a catastrophe be long postponed? It seemed to him as if the storm were nearly ripe; and it was so, more nearly than he thought.

He did not go to the cottage in the afternoon, withheld by fear and shame; but when dinner was over at Naseby House, and the Squire had gone off into a comfortable doze, Dick slipped out of the room, and ran across country, in part to save time, in part to save his own courage from growing cold; for he now hated the notion of the cottage or the Admiral, and if he did not hate, at least feared to think of Esther. He had no clue to her reflections; but he could not conceal from his own heart that he must have sunk in her esteem, and the spectacle of her infatuation galled him like an insult.

He knocked and was admitted. The room looked very much as on his last visit, with Esther at the table and Van Tromp beside the fire; but the expression of the two faces told a very different story. The girl was paler than usual; her eyes were dark, the colour seemed to have faded from round about them, and her swiftest glance was as intent as a stare. The appearance of the Admiral, on the other hand, was rosy, and flabby, and moist; his jowl hung over his shirt collar, his smile was loose and wandering, and he had so far relaxed the natural control of his eyes that one of them was aimed inward, as if to watch the growth of the carbuncle. We are warned against bad judgments; but the Admiral was certainly not sober. He made no attempt to rise when Richard entered, but waved his pipe flightily in the air, and gave a leer of welcome. Esther took as little notice of him as might be.

'Aha! Dick!' cried the painter. 'I've been to church; I have, upon my word. And I saw you there, though you didn't see me. And I saw a devilish pretty woman, by Gad. If it were not for this baldness, and a kind of crapulous air I can't disguise from myself – if it weren't for this and that and t'other thing – I – I've forgot what I was saying. Not that that matters, I've heaps of things to say. I'm in a communicative vein tonight. I'll let out all my cats, even unto seventy times seven. I'm in what I call *the* stage, and all I desire is a listener, although he were deaf, to be as happy as Nebuchadnezzar.'

Of the two hours which followed upon this it is unnecessary to give more than a sketch. The Admiral was extremely silly, now and then amusing, and never really offensive. It was plain that he kept in view the presence of his daughter, and chose subjects and a character of language that should not offend a lady. On almost any other occasion Dick would have enjoyed the scene. Van Tromp's egotism, flown with drink, struck a pitch above mere vanity. He became candid and explanatory; sought to take his auditors entirely into his confidence, and tell them his inmost conviction about himself. Between his self-knowledge, which was considerable, and his vanity, which was immense, he had created a strange hybrid animal, and called it by his own name. How he would plume his feathers over virtues which would have gladdened the heart of Caesar or St Paul; and, anon, complete his own portrait with one of those touches of pitiless realism which the satirist so often seeks in vain.

'Now, there's Dick,' he said, 'he's shrewd; he saw through me the first time we met, and told me so – told me so to my face, which I had the virtue to keep. I bear you no malice for it, Dick; you were right; I am a humbug.'

You may fancy how Esther quailed at this new feature of the meeting between her two idols.

And then, again, in a parenthesis:

'That,' said Van Tromp, 'was when I had to paint those dirty daubs of mine.'

And a little further on, laughingly said perhaps, but yet with an air of truth:

'I never had the slightest hesitation in sponging upon any human creature.'

Thereupon Dick got up.

'I think perhaps,' he said, 'we had better all be thinking of going to bed.' And he smiled with a feeble and deprecatory smile.

'Not at all,' cried the Admiral, 'I know a trick worth two of that. Puss here,' indicating his daughter, 'shall go to bed; and you and I will keep it up till all's blue.'

Thereupon Esther arose in sullen glory. She had sat and listened for two mortal hours while her idol defiled himself and sneered away his godhead. One by one, her illusions had departed. And now he wished to order her to bed in her own house! now he called her Puss! now, even as he uttered the words, toppling on his chair, he broke the stem of his tobacco pipe in three! Never did the sheep turn upon her shearer with a more commanding front. Her voice was calm, her enunciation a little slow, but perfectly distinct, and she stood before him as she spoke, in the simplest and most maidenly attitude.

'No,' she said, 'Mr Naseby will have the goodness to go home at once, and you will go to bed.'

The broken fragments of pipe fell from the Admiral's fingers; he seemed by his countenance to have lived too long in a world unworthy of him; but it is an odd circumstance, he attempted no reply, and sat thunderstruck, with open mouth.

Dick she motioned sharply towards the door, and he could only obey her. In the porch, finding she was close behind him, he ventured to pause and whisper, 'You have done right.'

'I have done as I pleased,' she said. 'Can he paint?'

'Many people like his paintings,' returned Dick, in stifled tones, 'I never did; I never said I did,' he added, fiercely defending himself before he was attacked.

'I ask you if he can paint. I will not be put off. *Can* he paint?' she repeated.

'No,' said Dick.

'Does he even like it?'

'Not now, I believe.'

'And he is drunk?' – she leaned upon the word with hatred.

'He has been drinking.'

'Go,' she said, and was turning to re-enter the house when another thought arrested her. 'Meet me tomorrow morning at the stile,' she said.

'I will,' replied Dick.

And then the door closed behind her, and Dick was alone in the darkness. There was still a chink of light above the sill, a warm, mild glow behind the window; the roof of the cottage and some of the banks and hazels were defined in denser darkness against the sky; but all else was formless, breathless, and noiseless like the pit. Dick remained as she had left him, standing squarely upon one foot and resting only on the toe of the other, and as he stood he listened with his soul. The sound of a chair pushed sharply over the floor startled his heart into his mouth; but the silence which had thus been disturbed settled back again at once upon the cottage and its vicinity. What took place during this interval is a secret from the world of men; but when it was over the voice of Esther spoke evenly and without interruption for perhaps half a minute, and as soon as that ceased heavy and uncertain footfalls crossed the parlour and mounted lurching up the stairs. The girl had tamed her father, Van Tromp had gone obediently to bed: so much was obvious to the watcher in the road. And yet he still waited, straining his ears, and with terror and sickness at his heart; for if Esther had followed her father, if she had even made one movement in this great conspiracy of men and nature to be still, Dick must have had instant knowledge of it from his station before the door; and if she had not moved, must she not have fainted? or might she not be dead?

He could hear the cottage clock deliberately measure out the seconds; time stood still with him; an almost superstitious terror took command of his faculties; at last, he could bear no more, and, springing through the little garden in two bounds, he put his face against the window. The blind, which had not been drawn fully down, left an open chink about an inch in height along the bottom of the glass, and the whole parlour was thus exposed to Dick's investigation. Esther sat upright at the table, her head resting on her hand, her eyes fixed upon the candle. Her brows were slightly bent, her mouth slightly open; her whole attitude so still and settled that Dick could hardly fancy that she breathed. She had not stirred at the sound of Dick's arrival. Soon after, making a considerable disturbance amid the vast silence of the night, the clock lifted up its voice, whined for a while like a partridge, and then eleven times hooted like a cuckoo. Still Esther continued immovable and gazed upon the candle. Midnight followed, and then one of the morning; and still she had not stirred, nor had Richard Naseby dared to quit the window. And then, about half past one, the candle she had been thus intently watching flared up into a last blaze of paper, and she leaped to her feet with an ejaculation, looked about her once, blew out the light, turned round, and was heard rapidly mounting the staircase in the dark.

Dick was left once more alone to darkness and to that dulled and dogged state of mind when a man thinks that

Misery must now have done her worst, and is almost glad to think so. He turned and walked slowly towards the stile; she had told him no hour, and he was determined, whenever she came, that she should find him waiting. As he got there the day began to dawn, and he leaned over a hurdle and beheld the shadows flee away. Up went the sun at last out of a bank of clouds that were already disbanding in the east; a herald wind had already sprung up to sweep the leafy earth and scatter the congregated dewdrops. 'Alas!' thought Dick Naseby, 'how can any other day come so distastefully to me?' He still wanted his experience of the morrow.

CHAPTER VII
THE ELOPEMENT

It was probably on the stroke of ten, and Dick had been half asleep for some time against the bank, when Esther came up the road carrying a bundle. Some kind of instinct, or perhaps the distant light footfalls, recalled him, while she was still a good way off, to the possession of his faculties, and he half raised himself and blinked upon the world. It took him some time to recollect his thoughts. He had awakened with a certain blank and childish sense of pleasure, like a man who had received a legacy overnight; but this feeling gradually died away, and was then suddenly and stunningly succeeded by a conviction of the truth. The whole story of the past night sprang into his mind with every detail, as by an exercise of the direct and speedy sense of sight, and he arose from the ditch and, with rueful courage, went to meet his love.

She came up to him walking steady and fast, her face still pale, but to all appearance perfectly composed; and she showed neither surprise, relief, nor pleasure at finding her lover on the spot. Nor did she offer him her hand.

'Here I am,' said he.

'Yes,' she replied; and then, without a pause or any change of voice, 'I want you to take me away,' she added.

'Away?' he repeated. 'How? Where?'

'Today,' she said. 'I do not care where it is, but I want you to take me away.'

'For how long? I do not understand,' gasped Dick.

'I shall never come back here any more,' was all she answered.

Wild words uttered, as these were, with perfect quiet of manner and voice, exercise a double influence on the hearer's mind. Dick was confounded; he recovered from astonishment only to fall into doubt and alarm. He looked upon her frozen attitude, so discouraging for a lover to behold, and recoiled from the thoughts which it suggested.

'To me?' he asked. 'Are you coming to me, Esther?'

'I want you to take me away,' she repeated with weary impatience. 'Take me away – take me away from here.'

The situation was not sufficiently defined. Dick asked himself with concern whether she were altogether in her right wits. To take her away, to marry her, to work off his hands for her support, Dick was content to do all this; yet he required some show of love upon her part. He was not one of those tough-hided and small-hearted males who would marry their love at the point of the bayonet rather than not marry her at all. He desired that a woman should come to his arms with an attractive willingness, if not with ardour. And Esther's bearing was more that of despair than that of love. It chilled him and taught him wisdom.

'Dearest,' he urged, 'tell me what you wish, and you shall have it; tell me your thoughts, and then I can advise you. But to go from here without a plan, without forethought, in the heat of a moment, is madder than madness, and can help nothing. I am not speaking like a man, but I speak the truth; and I tell you again, the thing's absurd, and wrong, and hurtful.'

She looked at him with a lowering, languid look of wrath.

'So you will not take me?' she said. 'Well, I will go alone.'

And she began to step forward on her way. But he threw himself before her.

'Esther, Esther!' he cried.

'Let me go – don't touch me – what right have you to interfere? Who are you, to touch me?' she flashed out, shrill with anger.

Then, being made bold by her violence, he took her firmly, almost roughly, by the arm, and held her while he spoke.

'You know well who I am, and what I am, and that I love you. You say I will not help you; but your heart knows the contrary. It is you who will not help me; for you will not tell me what you want. You see – or you could see, if you took the pains to look – how I have waited here all night to be ready at your service. I only asked information; I only urged you to consider; and I still urge and beg you to think better of your fancies. But if your mind is made up, so be it; I will beg no longer; I give you my orders; and I will not allow – not allow you to go hence alone.'

She looked at him for awhile with cold, unkind scrutiny, like one who tries the temper of a tool.

'Well, take me away, then,' she said with a sigh.

'Good,' said Dick. 'Come with me to the stables; there we shall get the pony-trap and drive to the junction. Tonight you shall be in London. I am yours so wholly that no words can make me more so; and, besides, you know it, and the words are needless. May God help me to be good to you, Esther – may God help me! for I see that you will not.'

So, without more speech, they set out together, and were already got some distance from the spot, ere he observed that she was still carrying the handbag. She gave it up to him, passively, but when he offered her his arm, merely shook her head and pursed up her lips. The sun shone clearly and pleasantly; the wind was fresh and brisk upon their faces, and smelt racily of woods and meadows. As they went down into the valley of the Thyme, the babble of the stream rose into the air like a perennial laughter. On the far-away hills, sunburst and shadow raced along the slopes and leaped from peak to peak. Earth, air and water, each seemed in better health and had more of the shrewd salt of life in them than upon ordinary mornings; and from east to west, from the lowest glen to the height of heaven, from every look and touch and scent, a human creature could gather the most encouraging intelligence as to the durability and spirit of the universe.

Through all this walked Esther, picking her small steps like a bird, but silent and with a cloud under her thick eyebrows. She seemed insensible, not only of nature, but of the presence of her companion. She was altogether engrossed in herself, and looked neither to right nor to left, but straight before her on the road. When they came to the bridge, however, she halted, leaned on the parapet, and stared for a moment at the clear, brown pool, and swift, transient snowdrift of the rapids.

'I am going to drink,' she said; and descended the winding footpath to the margin.

There she drank greedily in her hands and washed her temples with water. The coolness seemed to break, for an instant, the spell that lay upon her; for, instead of hastening forward again in her dull, indefatigable tramp, she stood still where she was, for near a minute, looking straight before her. And Dick, from above on the bridge where he stood to watch her, saw a strange, equivocal smile dawn slowly on her face and pass away again at once and suddenly, leaving her as grave as ever; and the sense of distance, which it is so cruel for a lover to endure, pressed with every moment more heavily on her companion. Her thoughts were all secret; her heart was locked and bolted; and he stood without, vainly wooing her with his eyes.

'Do you feel better?' asked Dick, as she at last rejoined him; and after the constraint of so long a silence, his voice sounded foreign to his own ears.

She looked at him for an appreciable fraction of a minute ere she answered, and when she did, it was in the monosyllable – 'Yes.'

Dick's solicitude was nipped and frosted. His words died away on his tongue. Even his eyes, despairing of encouragement, ceased to attend on hers. And they went on in silence through Kirton hamlet, where an old man followed them with his eyes, and perhaps envied them their youth and love; and across the Ivy beck where the mill was splashing and grumbling low thunder to itself in the chequered shadow of the dell, and the miller before the door was beating flour from his hands as he whistled a modulation; and up by the high spinney, whence they saw the mountains upon either hand; and down the hill again to the back courts and offices of Naseby House. Esther had kept ahead all the way, and Dick plodded obediently in her wake; but, as they neared the stables, he pushed on and took the lead. He would have preferred her to await him in the road while he went on and brought the carriage back, but after so many repulses and rebuffs he lacked courage to offer the suggestion. Perhaps, too, he felt it wiser to keep his convoy within sight. So they entered the yard in Indian file, like a tramp and his wife.

The groom's eyebrows rose as he received the order for the pony-phaeton, and kept rising during all his preparations. Esther stood bolt upright and looked steadily at some chickens in the corner of the yard. Master Richard himself, thought the groom, was not in his ordinary; for in truth, he carried the hand-bag like a talisman, and either stood listless, or set off suddenly walking in one direction after another with brisk, decisive footsteps. Moreover, he had apparently neglected to wash his hands, and bore the air of one returning from a prolonged nutting ramble. Upon the groom's countenance there began to grow up an expression as of one about to whistle. And hardly had the carriage turned the corner and rattled into the high road with this inexplicable pair than the whistle broke forth – prolonged, and low and tremulous; and the groom, already so far relieved, vented the rest of his surprise in one simple English word, friendly to the mouth of Jack-tar and the sooty pitman, and hurried to spread the news round the servants' hall of Naseby House. Luncheon would be on the table in little beyond an hour; and the Squire, on sitting down, would hardly fail to ask for Master Richard. Hence, as the intelligent reader can foresee, this groom has a part to play in the imbroglio.

Meantime, Dick had been thinking deeply and bitterly. It seemed to him as if his love had gone from him, indeed, yet gone but a little way; as if he needed but to find the right touch or intonation, and her heart would recognise him and be melted. Yet he durst not open his mouth, and drove in silence till they had passed the main park gates and turned into the cross-cut lane along the wall. Then it seemed to him as if it must be now, or never.

'Can't you see you are killing me?' he cried. 'Speak to me, look at me, treat me like a human man.'

She turned slowly and looked him in the face with eyes that seemed kinder. He dropped the reins and caught her hand, and she made no resistance, although her touch was unresponsive. But when, throwing one arm round her waist, he sought to kiss her lips, not like a lover indeed, not because he wanted to do so, but as a desperate man who puts his fortunes to the touch, she drew away from him with a knot in her forehead, backed and shied about fiercely with her head, and pushed him from her with her hand. Then there was no room left for doubt, and Dick saw, as clear as sunlight, that she had a distaste or nourished a grudge against him.

'Then you don't love me?' he said, drawing back from her, he also, as though her touch had burnt him; and then, as she made no answer, he repeated with another intonation, imperious and yet still pathetic, 'You don't love me, *do* you, *do* you?'

'I don't know,' she replied. 'Why do you ask me? Oh, how should I know? It has all been lies together – lies, and lies, and lies!'

He cried her name sharply, like a man who has taken a physical hurt, and that was the last word that either of them spoke until they reached Thymebury Junction.

This was a station isolated in the midst of moorlands, yet lying on the great up line to London. The nearest town, Thymebury itself, was seven miles distant along the branch they call the Vale of Thyme Railway. It was now nearly half an hour past noon, the down train had just gone by, and there would be no more traffic at the junction until half past three, when the local train comes in to meet the up express at a quarter before four. The stationmaster had already gone off to his garden, which was half a mile away in a hollow of the moor; a porter, who was just leaving, took charge of the phaeton, and promised to return it before night to Naseby House; only a deaf, snuffy, and stern old man remained to play propriety for Dick and Esther.

Before the phaeton had driven off, the girl had entered the station and seated herself upon a bench. The endless, empty moorlands stretched before her, entirely unenclosed, and with no boundary but the horizon. Two lines of rails, a waggon shed, and a few telegraph posts, alone diversified the outlook. As for sounds, the silence was unbroken save by the chant of the telegraph wires and the crying of the plovers on the waste. With the approach of midday the wind had more and more fallen; it was now sweltering hot and the air trembled in the sunshine.

Dick paused for an instant on the threshold of the platform. Then, in two steps, he was by her side and speaking almost with a sob.

'Esther,' he said, 'have pity on me. What have I done? Can you not forgive me? Esther, you loved me once – can you not love me still?'

'How can I tell you? How am I to know?' she answered. 'You are all a lie to me – all a lie from first to last. You were laughing at my folly, playing with me like a child, at the very time when you declared you loved me. Which was true? was any of it true? or was it all, all a mockery? I am weary trying to find out. And you say I loved you; I loved my father's friend. I never loved, I never heard of, you, until that man came home and I began to find myself deceived. Give me back my father, be what you were before, and you may talk of love indeed!'

'Then you cannot forgive me – cannot?' he asked.

'I have nothing to forgive,' she answered. 'You do not understand.'

'Is that your last word, Esther?' said he, very white, and biting his lip to keep it still.

'Yes, that is my last word,' replied she.

'Then we are here on false pretences, and we stay here no longer,' he said. 'Had you still loved me, right or wrong, I should have taken you away, because then I could have made you happy. But as it is – I must speak plainly – what you propose is degrading to you, and an insult to me, and a rank unkindness to your father. Your father may be this or that, but you should use him like a fellow creature.'

'What do you mean?' she flashed. 'I leave him my house and all my money; it is more than he deserves. I wonder you dare speak to me about that man. And besides, it is all he cares for; let him take it, and let me never hear from him again.'

'I thought you romantic about fathers,' he said.

'Is that a taunt?' she demanded.

'No,' he replied, 'it is an argument. No one can make you like him, but don't disgrace him in his own eyes. He is old, Esther, old and broken down. Even I am sorry for him, and he has been the loss of all I cared for. Write to your aunt; when I see her answer you can leave quietly and naturally, and I will take you to your aunt's door. But in the meantime you must go home. You have no money, and so you are helpless, and must do as I tell you; and believe me, Esther, I do all for your good, and your good only, so God help me.'

She had put her hand into her pocket and withdrawn it empty.

'I counted upon you,' she wailed.

'You counted rightly then,' he retorted. 'I will not, to please you for a moment, make both of us unhappy for our lives; and, since I cannot marry you, we have only been too long away, and must go home at once.'

'Dick,' she cried suddenly, 'perhaps I might – perhaps in time – perhaps – '

'There is no perhaps about the matter,' interrupted Dick. 'I must go and bring the phaeton.' And with that he strode from the station, all in a glow of passion and virtue. Esther, whose eyes had come alive and her cheeks flushed during these last words, relapsed in a second into a state of petrifaction. She remained without motion during his absence, and, when he returned, suffered herself to be put back into the phaeton, and driven off on the return journey like an idiot or a tired child. Compared with what she was now, her condition of the morning seemed positively natural. She sat white and cold and silent, and there was no speculation in her eyes. Poor Dick flailed and flailed at the pony, and once tried to whistle, but his courage was going down; huge clouds of despair gathered together in his soul, and from time to time their darkness was divided by a piercing flash of longing and regret. He had lost his love – he had lost his love for good.

The pony was tired, and the hills very long and steep, and the air sultrier than ever, for now the breeze began to fail entirely. It seemed as if this miserable drive would never be done, as if poor Dick would never be able to go away and be comfortably wretched by himself; for all his desire was to escape from her presence and the reproach of her averted looks. He had lost his love, he thought – he had lost his love for good.

They were already not far from the cottage, when his heart again faltered and he appealed to her once more, speaking low and eagerly in broken phrases.

'I cannot live without your love,' he concluded.

'I do not understand what you mean,' she replied, and I believe with perfect truth.

'Then,' said he, wounded to the quick, 'your aunt might come and fetch you herself. Of course you can command me as you please. But I think it would be better so.'

'Oh yes,' she said wearily, 'better so.'

This was the only exchange of words between them till about four o'clock; the phaeton, mounting the lane, 'opened out' the cottage between the leafy banks. Thin smoke went straight up from the chimney; the flowers in the garden, the hawthorn in the lane, hung down their heads in the heat; the stillness was broken only by the sound of hoofs. For right before the gate a livery servant rode slowly up and down, leading a saddle horse. And in this last Dick shuddered to identify his father's chestnut.

Alas! poor Richard, what should this portend?

The servant, as in duty bound, dismounted and took the phaeton into his keeping; yet Dick thought he touched his hat to him with something of a grin. Esther, passive as ever, was helped out and crossed the garden with a slow and mechanical gait; and Dick, following close behind her, heard from within the cottage his father's voice upraised in anathema, and the shriller tones of the Admiral responding in the key of war.

Squire Naseby, on sitting down to lunch, had enquired for Dick, whom he had not seen since the day before at dinner; and the servant answering awkwardly that Master Richard had come back but had gone out again with the pony-phaeton, his suspicions became aroused, and he cross-questioned the man until the whole was out. It appeared from this report that Dick had been going about for nearly a month with a girl in the Vale – a Miss Van Tromp; that she lived near Lord Trevanion's upper wood; that recently Miss Van Tromp's papa had returned home from foreign parts after a prolonged absence; that this papa was an old gentleman, very chatty and free with his money in the public house – whereupon Mr Naseby's face became encrimsoned; that the papa, furthermore, was said to be an admiral – whereupon Mr Naseby spat out a whistle brief and fierce as an oath; that Master Dick seemed very friendly with the papa – 'God help him!' said Mr Naseby; that last night Master Dick had not come in, and today he had driven away in the phaeton with the young lady –

'Young woman,' corrected Mr Naseby.

'Yes, sir,' said the man, who had been unwilling enough to gossip from the first, and was now cowed by the effect of his communications on the master. 'Young woman, sir!'

'Had they luggage?' demanded the Squire.

'Yes, sir.'

Mr Naseby was silent for a moment, struggling to keep down his emotion, and he mastered it so far as to mount into the sarcastic vein, when he was in the nearest danger of melting into the sorrowful.

'And was this – this Van Dunk with them?' he asked, dwelling scornfully upon the name.

The servant believed not, and being eager to shift the responsibility of speech to other shoulders, suggested that perhaps the master had better inquire further from George the stableman in person.

'Tell him to saddle the chestnut and come with me. He can take the gray gelding; for we may ride fast. And then you can take away this trash,' added Mr Naseby, pointing to the luncheon; and he arose, lordly in his anger, and marched forth upon the terrace to await his horse.

There Dick's old nurse shrunk up to him, for the news went like wildfire over Naseby House, and timidly expressed a hope that there was nothing much amiss with the young master.

'I'll pull him through,' the Squire said grimly, as though he meant to pull him through a threshing-mill, 'I'll save him from this gang; God help him with the next! He has a taste for low company, and no natural affections to steady him. His father was no society for him; he must go fuddling with a Dutchman, Nance, and now he's caught. Let us pray he'll take the lesson,' he added more gravely, 'but youth is here to make troubles, and age to pull them out again.'

Nance whimpered and recalled several episodes of Dick's childhood, which moved Mr Naseby to blow his nose and shake her hard by the hand; and then, the horse arriving opportunely, to get himself without delay into the saddle and canter off.

He rode straight, hot spur, to Thymebury, where, as was to be expected, he could glean no tidings of the runaways. They had not been seen at the George; they had not been seen at the station. The shadow darkened on Mr Naseby's face; the junction did not occur to him; his last hope was for Van Tromp's cottage; thither he bade George guide him, and thither he followed, nursing grief, anxiety, and indignation in his heart.

'Here it is, sir,' said George stopping.

'What! on my own land!' he cried. 'How's this? I let this place to somebody – M'Whirter or M'Glashan.'

'Miss M'Glashan was the young lady's aunt, sir, I believe,' returned George.

'Ay – dummies,' said the Squire. 'I shall whistle for my rent too. Here, take my horse.'

The Admiral, this hot afternoon, was sitting by the window with a long glass. He already knew the Squire by sight, and now, seeing him dismount before the cottage and come striding through the garden, concluded without doubt he was there to ask for Esther's hand.

'This is why the girl is not yet home,' he thought: 'a very suitable delicacy on young Naseby's part.'

And he composed himself with some pomp, answered the loud rattle of the riding whip upon the door with a dulcet invitation to enter, and coming forward with a bow and a smile, 'Mr Naseby, I believe?' said he.

The Squire came armed for battle; took in his man from top to toe in one rapid and scornful glance, and decided on a course at once. He must let the fellow see that he understood him.

'You are Mr Van Tromp?' he returned roughly, and without taking any notice of the proffered hand.

'The same, sir,' replied the Admiral. 'Pray be seated.'

'No sir,' said the Squire, point-blank, 'I will not be seated. I am told that you are an admiral,' he added.

'No sir, I am not an admiral,' returned Van Tromp, who now began to grow nettled and enter into the spirit of the interview.

'Then why do you call yourself one, sir?'

'I have to ask your pardon, I do not,' says Van Tromp, as grand as the Pope.

But nothing was of avail against the Squire.

'You sail under false colours from beginning to end,' he said. 'Your very house was taken under a sham name.'

'It is not my house. I am my daughter's guest,' replied the Admiral. 'If it *were* my house – '

'Well?' said the Squire, 'what then? hey?'

The Admiral looked at him nobly, but was silent.

'Look here,' said Mr. Naseby, 'this intimidation is a waste of time; it is thrown away on me, sir; it will not succeed with me. I will not permit you even to gain time by your fencing. Now, sir, I presume you understand what brings me here.'

'I am entirely at a loss to account for your intrusion,' bows and waves Van Tromp.

'I will try to tell you then. I come here as a father' – down came the riding whip upon the table – 'I have right and justice upon my side. I understand your calculations, but you calculated without me. I am a man of the world, and I see through you and your manoeuvres. I am dealing now with a conspiracy – I stigmatise it as such, and I will expose it and crush it. And now I order you to tell me how far things have gone, and whither you have smuggled my unhappy son.'

'My God, sir!' Van Tromp broke out, 'I have had about enough of this. Your son? God knows where he is for me! What the devil have I to do with your son? My daughter is out, for the matter of that; I might ask you where she was, and what would you say to that? But this is all midsummer madness. Name your business distinctly, and be off.'

'How often am I to tell you?' cried the Squire. 'Where did your daughter take my son today in that cursed pony-carriage?'

'In a pony-carriage?' repeated Van Tromp.

'Yes, sir – with luggage.'

'Luggage?' – Van Tromp had turned a little pale.

'Luggage, I said – luggage!' shouted Naseby. 'You may spare me this dissimulation. Where's my son? You are speaking to a father, sir, a father.'

'But, sir, if this be true,' out came Van Tromp in a new key, 'it is I who have an explanation to demand?'

'Precisely. There is the conspiracy,' retorted Naseby. 'Oh!' he added, 'I am a man of the world. I can see through and through you.'

Van Tromp began to understand.

'You speak a great deal about being a father, Mr Naseby,' said he, 'I believe you forget that the appellation is common to both of us. I am at a loss to figure to myself, however dimly, how any man – I have not said any gentleman – could so brazenly insult another as you have been insulting me since you entered this house. For the first time I appreciate your base insinuations, and I despise them and you. You were, I am told, a manufacturer; I am an artist; I have seen better days; I have moved in societies where you would not be received, and dined where you would be glad to pay a pound to see me dining. The so-called aristocracy of wealth, sir, I despise. I refuse to help you; I refuse to be helped by you. There lies the door.'

And the Admiral stood forth in a halo.

It was then that Dick entered. He had been waiting in the porch for some time back, and Esther had been listlessly standing by his side. He had put out his hand to bar her entrance, and she had submitted without surprise; and though she seemed to listen, she scarcely appeared to comprehend. Dick, on his part, was as white as a sheet; his eyes burned and his lips trembled with anger as he thrust the door suddenly

63

open, introduced Esther with ceremonious gallantry, and stood forward and knocked his hat firmer on his head like a man about to leap.

'What is all this?' he demanded.

'Is this your father, Mr Naseby?' inquired the Admiral.

'It is,' said the young man.

'I make you my compliments,' returned Van Tromp.

'Dick!' cried his father, suddenly breaking forth, 'it is not too late, is it? I have come here in time to save you. Come, come away with me – come away from this place.'

And he fawned upon Dick with his hands.

'Keep your hands off me,' cried Dick, not meaning unkindness, but because his nerves were shattered by so many successive miseries.

'No, no,' said the old man, 'don't repulse your father, Dick, when he has come here to save you. Don't repulse me, my boy. Perhaps I have not been kind to you, not quite considerate, too harsh; my boy, it was not for want of love. Think of old times. I was kind to you then, was I not? When you were a child, and your mother was with us.' Mr Naseby was interrupted by a sort of sob. Dick stood looking at him in amaze. 'Come away,' pursued the father in a whisper, 'you need not be afraid of any consequences. I am a man of the world, Dick; and she can have no claim on you – no claim, I tell you; and we'll be handsome too, Dick – we'll give them a good round figure, father and daughter, and there's an end.'

He had been trying to get Dick towards the door, but the latter stood off.

'You had better take care, sir, how you insult that lady,' said the son, as black as night.

'You would not choose between your father and your mistress?' said the father.

'What do you call her, sir?' cried Dick, high and clear.

Forbearance and patience were not among Mr Naseby's qualities.

'I called her your mistress,' he shouted, 'and I might have called her a – '

'That is an unmanly lie,' replied Dick, slowly.

'Dick!' cried the father, 'Dick!'

'I do not care,' said the son, strengthening himself against his own heart, 'I – I have said it, and it is the truth.'

There was a pause.

'Dick,' said the old man at last, in a voice that was shaken as by a gale of wind, 'I am going. I leave you with your friends, sir – with your friends. I came to serve you, and now I go away a broken man. For years I have seen this coming, and now it has come. You never loved me. Now you have been the death of me. You may boast of that. Now I leave you. God pardon you.'

With that he was gone; and the three who remained together heard his horse's hoofs descend the lane. Esther had not made a sign throughout the interview, and still kept silence now that it was over; but the Admiral, who had once or twice moved forward and drawn back again, now advanced for good.

'You are a man of spirit, sir,' said he to Dick, 'but though I am no friend to parental interference, I will say that you were heavy on the governor.' Then he added with a chuckle: 'You began, Richard, with a silver spoon, and here you are in the water like the rest. Work, work, nothing like work. You have parts, you have manners; why, with application you may die a millionaire!'

Dick shook himself. He took Esther by the hand, looking at her mournfully.

'Then this is farewell,' he said.

'Yes,' she answered. There was no tone in her voice, and she did not return his gaze.

'For ever,' added Dick.

'For ever,' she repeated mechanically.

'I have had hard measure,' he continued. 'In time I believe I could have shown you I was worthy, and there was no time long enough to show how much I loved you. But it was not to be. I have lost all.'

He relinquished her hand, still looking at her, and she turned to leave the room.

'Why, what in fortune's name is the meaning of all this?' cried Van Tromp. 'Esther come back!'

'Let her go,' said Dick, and he watched her disappear with strangely mingled feelings. For he had fallen into that stage when men have the vertigo of misfortune, court the strokes of destiny, and rush towards anything decisive, that it may free them from suspense though at the cost of ruin. It is one of the many minor forms of suicide.

'She did not love me,' he said, turning to her father.

'I feared as much,' said he, 'when I sounded her. Poor Dick, poor Dick. And yet I believe I am as much cut up as you are. I was born to see others happy.'

'You forget,' returned Dick, with something like a sneer, 'that I am now a pauper.'

Van Tromp snapped his fingers.

'Tut!' said he, 'Esther has plenty for us all.'

Dick looked at him with some wonder. It had never dawned upon him that this shiftless, thriftless, worthless, sponging parasite was yet, after and in spite of all, not mercenary in the issue of his thoughts; yet so it was.

'Now,' said Dick, 'I must go.'

'Go?' cried Van Tromp. 'Where? Not one foot, Mr Richard Naseby. Here you shall stay in the meantime! and – well, and do something practical – advertise for a situation as private secretary – and when you have it, go and welcome. But in the meantime, sir, no false pride; we must stay with our friends; we must sponge a while on Papa Van Tromp, who has sponged so often upon us.'

'By God,' cried Dick, 'I believe you are the best of the lot.'

'Dick, my boy,' replied the Admiral, winking, 'you mark me, I am not the worst.'

'Then why,' began Dick, and then paused. 'But Esther,' he began again, once more to interrupt himself. 'The fact is, Admiral,' he came out with it roundly now, 'your daughter wished to run away from you today, and I only brought her back with difficulty.'

'In the pony-carriage?' asked the Admiral, with the silliness of extreme surprise.

'Yes,' Dick answered.

'Why, what the devil was she running away from?'

Dick found the question unusually hard to answer.

'Why,' said he, 'you know, you're a bit of a rip.'

'I behave to that girl, sir, like an archdeacon,' replied Van Tromp warmly.

'Well – excuse me – but you know you drink,' insisted Dick.

'I know that I was a sheet in the wind's eye, sir, once – once only, since I reached this place,' retorted the Admiral. 'And even then I was fit for any drawing room. I should like you to tell me how many fathers, lay and clerical, go upstairs every day with a face like a lobster and cod's eyes – and are dull, upon the back of it – not even mirth for the money! No, if that's what she runs for, all I say is, let her run.'

'You see,' Dick tried it again, 'she has fancies – '

67

'Confound her fancies!' cried Van Tromp. 'I used her kindly; she had her own way; I was her father. Besides, I had taken quite a liking to the girl, and meant to stay with her for good. But I tell you what it is, Dick, since she has trifled with you – oh, yes, she did though! – and since her old papa's not good enough for her – the devil take her, say I.'

'You will be kind to her at least?' said Dick.

'I never was unkind to a living soul,' replied the Admiral. 'Firm I can be, but not unkind.'

'Well,' said Dick, offering his hand, 'God bless you, and farewell.'

The Admiral swore by all his gods he should not go. 'Dick,' he said, 'you are a selfish dog; you forget your old Admiral. You wouldn't leave him alone, would you?'

It was useless to remind him that the house was not his to dispose of, that being a class of considerations to which his intelligence was closed; so Dick tore himself off by force, and, shouting a goodbye, made off along the lane to Thymebury.

CHAPTER IX
IN WHICH THE LIBERAL EDITOR
REAPPEARS AS 'DEUX EX MACHINA'

It was perhaps a week later, as old Mr Naseby sat brooding in his study, that there was shown in upon him, on urgent business, a little hectic gentleman shabbily attired.

'I have to ask pardon for this intrusion, Mr Naseby,' he said, 'but I come here to perform a duty. My card has been sent in, but perhaps you may not know, what it does not tell you, that I am the editor of the *Thymebury Star*.'

Mr Naseby looked up, indignant.

'I cannot fancy,' he said, 'that we have much in common to discuss.'

'I have only a word to say – one piece of information to communicate. Some months ago, we had – you will pardon my referring to it, it is absolutely necessary – but we had an unfortunate difference as to facts.'

'Have you come to apologise?' asked the Squire, sternly.

'No, sir; to mention a circumstance. On the morning in question, your son, Mr Richard Naseby – '

'I do not permit his name to be mentioned.'

'You will, however, permit me,' replied the editor.

'You are cruel,' said the Squire. He was right, he was a broken man.

Then the editor described Dick's warning visit; and how he had seen in the lad's eye that there was a thrashing in the wind, and had escaped through pity only – so the editor put it – 'through pity only sir. And oh, sir,' he went on, 'if you had seen him speaking up for you, I am sure you would have been proud of your son. I know I admired the lad myself, and indeed that's what brings me here.'

'I have misjudged him,' said the Squire. 'Do you know where he is?'

'Yes, sir, he lies sick at Thymebury.'

'You can take me to him?'

'I can.'

'I pray God he may forgive me,' said the father.

And he and the editor made post-haste for the country town.

Next day the report went abroad that Mr Richard was reconciled to his father and had been taken home to Naseby House. He was still ailing, it was said, and the Squire nursed him like the proverbial woman. Rumour, in this instance, did no more than justice to the truth; and over the sickbed many confidences were exchanged, and clouds that had been growing for years passed away in a few hours, and, as fond mankind loves to hope, for ever. Many long talks had been fruitless in external action, though fruitful for the understanding of the pair; but at last, one showery Tuesday, the Squire might have been observed upon his way to the cottage in the lane.

The old gentleman had arranged his features with a view to self-command, rather than external cheerfulness; and he entered the cottage on his visit of conciliation with the bearing of a clergyman come to announce a death.

The Admiral and his daughter were both within, and both looked upon their visitor with more surprise than favour.

'Sir,' said he to Van Tromp, 'I am told I have done you much injustice.'

There came a little sound in Esther's throat, and she put her hand suddenly to her heart.

'You have, sir; and the acknowledgment suffices,' replied the Admiral. 'I am prepared, sir, to be easy with you, since I hear you have made it up with my friend Dick. But let me remind you that you owe some apologies to this young lady also.'

'I shall have the temerity to ask for more than her forgiveness,' said the Squire. 'Miss Van Tromp,' he continued, 'once I was in great distress, and knew nothing of you or your character; but I believe you will pardon a few rough words to an old man who asks forgiveness from his heart. I have heard much of you since then; for you have a fervent advocate in my house. I believe you will understand that I speak of my son. He is, I regret to say, very far from well; he does not pick up as the doctors had expected; he has a great deal upon his mind, and, to tell you the truth, my girl, if you won't help us, I am afraid I shall lose him. Come now, forgive him! I was angry with him once myself, and I found I was in the wrong. This is only a misunderstanding, like the other, believe me; and with one kind movement, you may give happiness to him, and to me, and to yourself.'

Esther made a movement towards the door, but long before she reached it she had broken forth sobbing.

'It is all right,' said the Admiral, 'I understand the sex. Let me make you my compliments, Mr Naseby.'

The Squire was too much relieved to be angry.

'My dear,' said he to Esther, 'you must not agitate yourself.'

'She had better go up and see him right away,' suggested Van Tromp.

'I had not ventured to propose it,' replied the Squire. '*Les convenances*, I believe – '

'*Je m'en fiche*,' cried the Admiral, snapping his fingers. 'She shall go and see my friend Dick. Run and get ready, Esther.'

Esther obeyed.

'She has not – has not run away again?' inquired Mr Naseby, as soon as she was gone.

'No,' said Van Tromp, 'not again. She is a devilish odd girl though, mind you that.'

'But I cannot stomach the man with the carbuncles,' thought the Squire.

And this is why there is a new household and a brand new baby in Naseby Dower House; and why the great Van Tromp lives in pleasant style upon the shores of England; and why twenty-six individual copies of the *Thymebury Star* are received daily at the door of Naseby House.

The Body Snatcher

Every night in the year, four of us sat in the small parlour of the George at Debenham – the undertaker, and the landlord, and Fettes, and myself. Sometimes there would be more; but blow high, blow low, come rain or snow or frost, we four would be each planted in his own particular armchair. Fettes was an old drunken Scotchman, a man of education obviously, and a man of some property, since he lived in idleness. He had come to Debenham years ago, while still young, and by a mere continuance of living had grown to be an adopted townsman. His blue camlet cloak was a local antiquity, like the church spire. His place in the parlour at the George, his absence from church, his old, crapulous, disreputable vices, were all things of course in Debenham. He had some vague radical opinions and some fleeting infidelities, which he would now and again set forth and emphasise with tottering slaps upon the table. He drank rum – five glasses regularly every evening; and for the greater portion of his nightly visit to the George sat, with his glass in his right hand, in a state of melancholy alcoholic saturation. We called him the doctor, for he was supposed to have some special knowledge of medicine, and had been known, upon a pinch, to set a fracture or reduce a dislocation; but beyond these slight particulars, we had no knowledge of his character and antecedents.

One dark winter night – it had struck nine some time before the landlord joined us – there was a sick man in the George, a great neighbouring proprietor suddenly struck down with apoplexy on his way to Parliament; and the great man's still greater London doctor had been telegraphed to his bedside. It was the first time that such a thing had happened in Debenham, for the railway was but newly open, and we were all proportionately moved by the occurrence.

'He's come,' said the landlord, after he had filled and lighted his pipe.

'He?' said I. 'Who? – not the doctor?'

'Himself,' replied our host.

'What is his name?'

'Doctor Macfarlane,' said the landlord.

Fettes was far through his third tumbler, stupidly fuddled, now nodding over, now staring mazily around him; but at the last word he seemed to awaken, and repeated the name 'Macfarlane' twice, quietly enough the first time, but with sudden emotion at the second.

'Yes,' said the landlord, 'that's his name, Doctor Wolfe Macfarlane.'

Fettes became instantly sober; his eyes awoke, his voice became clear, loud, and steady, his language forcible and earnest. We were all startled by the transformation, as if a man had risen from the dead.

'I beg your pardon,' he said, 'I am afraid I have not been paying much attention to your talk. Who is this Wolfe Macfarlane?' And then, when he had heard the landlord out, 'It cannot be, it cannot be,' he added, 'and yet I would like well to see him face to face.'

'Do you know him, doctor?' asked the undertaker, with a gasp.

'God forbid!' was the reply. 'And yet the name is a strange one; it were too much to fancy two. Tell me, landlord, is he old?'

'Well,' said the host, 'he's not a young man, to be sure, and his hair is white; but he looks younger than you.'

'He is older, though; years older. But,' with a slap upon the table, 'it's the rum you see in my face – rum and sin. This man, perhaps, may have an easy conscience and a good digestion. Conscience! Hear me speak. You would think I was some good, old, decent Christian, would you not? But no, not I;

I never canted. Voltaire might have canted if he'd stood in my shoes; but the brains' – with a rattling fillip on his bald head – 'the brains were clear and active, and I saw and made no deductions.'

'If you know this doctor,' I ventured to remark, after a somewhat awful pause, 'I should gather that you do not share the landlord's good opinion.'

Fettes paid no regard to me.

'Yes,' he said, with sudden decision, 'I must see him face to face.'

There was another pause, and then a door was closed rather sharply on the first floor, and a step was heard upon the stair.

'That's the doctor,' cried the landlord. 'Look sharp, and you can catch him.'

It was but two steps from the small parlour to the door of the old George Inn; the wide oak staircase landed almost in the street; there was room for a Turkey rug and nothing more between the threshold and the last round of the descent; but this little space was every evening brilliantly lit up, not only by the light upon the stair and the great signal lamp below the sign, but by the warm radiance of the bar-room window. The George thus brightly advertised itself to passers-by in the cold street. Fettes walked steadily to the spot, and we, who were hanging behind, beheld the two men meet, as one of them had phrased it, face to face. Dr Macfarlane was alert and vigorous. His white hair set off his pale and placid, although energetic, countenance. He was richly dressed in the finest of broadcloth and the whitest of linen, with a great gold watch chain, and studs and spectacles of the same precious material. He wore a broad folded tie, white and speckled with lilac, and he carried on his arm a comfortable driving coat of fur. There was no doubt but he became his years, breathing, as he did, of wealth and consideration; and it was a surprising contrast to see our parlour sot – bald, dirty, pimpled, and robed in his old camlet cloak – confront him at the bottom of the stairs.

'Macfarlane!' he said somewhat loudly, more like a herald than a friend.

The great doctor pulled up short on the fourth step, as though the familiarity of the address surprised and somewhat shocked his dignity.

'Toddy Macfarlane!' repeated Fettes.

The London man almost staggered. He stared for the swiftest of seconds at the man before him, glanced behind him with a sort of scare, and then in a startled whisper, 'Fettes!' he said, 'you!'

'Ay,' said the other, 'me! Did you think I was dead too? We are not so easy shut of our acquaintance.'

'Hush, hush!' exclaimed the doctor. 'Hush, hush! This meeting is so unexpected – I can see you are unmanned. I hardly knew you, I confess, at first; but I am overjoyed – overjoyed to have this opportunity. For the present it must be how-d'ye-do and goodbye in one, for my fly is waiting, and I must not fail the train; but you shall – let me see – yes – you shall give me your address, and you can count on early news of me. We must do something for you, Fettes. I fear you are out at elbows; but we must see to that for auld lang syne, as once we sang at suppers.'

'Money!' cried Fettes, 'money from you! The money that I had from you is lying where I cast it in the rain.'

Dr Macfarlane had talked himself into some measure of superiority and confidence, but the uncommon energy of this refusal cast him back into his first confusion.

A horrible, ugly look came and went across his almost venerable countenance. 'My dear fellow,' he said, 'be it as you please; my last thought is to offend you. I would intrude on none. I will leave you my address, however – '

'I do not wish it – I do not wish to know the roof that shelters you,' interrupted the other. 'I heard your name; I feared it might be you; I wished to know if, after all, there were a God; I know now that there is none. Begone!'

He still stood in the middle of the rug, between the stair and doorway; and the great London physician, in order to escape, would be forced to step to one side. It was plain that he hesitated before the thought of this humiliation. White as he was, there was a dangerous glitter in his spectacles; but while he still paused uncertain, he became aware that the driver of his fly was peering in from the street at this unusual scene and caught a glimpse at the same time of our little body from the parlour, huddled by the corner of the bar. The presence of so many witnesses decided him at once to flee. He crouched together, brushing on the wainscot, and made a dart like a serpent, striking for the door. But his tribulation was not yet entirely at an end, for even as he was passing Fettes clutched him by the arm and these words came in a whisper, and yet painfully distinct, 'Have you seen it again?'

The great rich London doctor cried out aloud with a sharp, throttling cry; he dashed his questioner across the open space, and, with his hands over his head, fled out of the door like a detected thief. Before it had occurred to one of us to make a movement the fly was already rattling toward the station. The scene was over like a dream, but the dream had left proofs and traces of its passage. Next day the servant found the fine gold spectacles broken on the threshold, and that very night we were all standing breathless by the bar-room window, and Fettes at our side, sober, pale, and resolute in look.

'God protect us, Mr Fettes!' said the landlord, coming first into possession of his customary senses. 'What in the universe is all this? These are strange things you have been saying.'

Fettes turned toward us; he looked us each in succession in the face. 'See if you can hold your tongues,' said he. 'That man Macfarlane is not safe to cross; those that have done so already have repented it too late.'

And then, without so much as finishing his third glass, far less waiting for the other two, he bade us goodbye and went forth, under the lamp of the hotel, into the black night.

We three turned to our places in the parlour, with the big red fire and four clear candles; and as we recapitulated what had passed, the first chill of our surprise soon changed into a glow of curiosity. We sat late; it was the latest session I have known in the old George. Each man, before we parted, had his theory that he was bound to prove; and none of us had any nearer business in this world than to track out the past of our condemned companion, and surprise the secret that he shared with the great London doctor. It is no great boast, but I believe I was a better hand at worming out a story than either of my fellows at the George; and perhaps there is now no other man alive who could narrate to you the following foul and unnatural events.

In his young days Fettes studied medicine in the schools of Edinburgh. He had talent of a kind, the talent that picks up swiftly what it hears and readily retails it for its own. He worked little at home; but he was civil, attentive, and intelligent in the presence of his masters. They soon picked him out as a lad who listened closely and remembered well; nay, strange as it seemed to me when I first heard it, he was in those days well favoured, and pleased by his exterior. There was, at that period, a certain extramural teacher of anatomy, whom I shall here designate by the letter K. His name was subsequently too well known. The man who bore it skulked through the streets of Edinburgh in disguise, while the mob that applauded at the execution of Burke called loudly for the blood of his employer. But Mr K was then at the top of his vogue; he enjoyed a popularity due partly to his own talent and address, partly to the incapacity of his rival, the university professor. The students, at least, swore by his name, and Fettes believed himself, and was believed by others, to have laid the foundations of success when he had acquired the favour of this meteorically famous man. Mr K was a *bon vivant* as well as an accomplished teacher; he liked a sly illusion no less than a careful preparation. In both capacities Fettes enjoyed and deserved his notice, and by the second year of his attendance he held the half-regular position of second demonstrator or sub-assistant in his class.

In this capacity the charge of the theatre and lecture room devolved in particular upon his shoulders. He had to answer for the cleanliness of the premises and the conduct of the other students, and it was a part of his duty to supply, receive, and divide the various subjects. It was with a view to this last – at that time very delicate – affair that he was lodged by Mr K in the same wynd, and at last in the same building, with the dissecting rooms. Here, after a night of turbulent pleasures, his hand still tottering, his sight still misty and confused, he would be called out of bed in the black hours before the winter dawn by the unclean and desperate interlopers who supplied the table. He would open the door to these men, since infamous throughout the land. He would help them with their tragic burden, pay them their sordid price, and remain alone, when they were gone, with the unfriendly relics of humanity. From such a scene he would return to snatch another hour or two of slumber, to repair the abuses of the night, and refresh himself for the labours of the day.

Few lads could have been more insensible to the impressions of a life thus passed among the ensigns of mortality. His mind was closed against all general considerations. He was incapable of interest in the fate and fortunes of another, the slave of his own desires and low ambitions. Cold, light, and selfish in the last resort, he had that modicum of prudence, miscalled morality, which keeps a man from inconvenient drunkenness or punishable theft. He coveted, besides, a measure of consideration from his masters and his fellow pupils, and he had no desire to fail conspicuously in the external parts of life. Thus he made it his pleasure to gain some distinction in his studies, and day after day rendered unimpeachable eye-service to his employer, Mr K. For his day of work he indemnified himself by nights of roaring, blackguardly enjoyment; and when that balance had been struck, the organ that he called his conscience declared itself content.

The supply of subjects was a continual trouble to him as well as to his master. In that large and busy class, the raw material of the anatomists kept perpetually running out; and the business thus rendered necessary was not only unpleasant in itself, but threatened dangerous consequences to all who were concerned. It was the policy of Mr K to ask no questions in his dealings with the trade. 'They bring the body, and we pay the price,' he used to say, dwelling on the alliteration – '*quid pro quo*'. And, again, and somewhat profanely, 'Ask no questions,' he would tell his assistants, 'for conscience' sake.' There was no understanding that the subjects were provided by the crime of murder. Had that idea been broached to him in words, he would have recoiled in horror; but the lightness of his speech upon so grave a matter

was, in itself, an offence against good manners, and a tempta-
tion to the men with whom he dealt. Fettes, for instance, had
often remarked to himself upon the singular freshness of
the bodies. He had been struck again and again by the hang-
dog, abominable looks of the ruffians who came to him before
the dawn; and, putting things together clearly in his private
thoughts, he perhaps attributed a meaning too immoral and
too categorical to the unguarded counsels of his master. He
understood his duty, in short, to have three branches: to take
what was brought, to pay the price, and to avert the eye from
any evidence of crime.

One November morning this policy of silence was put
sharply to the test. He had been awake all night with a racking
toothache – pacing his room like a caged beast or throwing
himself in fury on his bed – and had fallen at last into that
profound, uneasy slumber that so often follows on a night of
pain, when he was awakened by the third or fourth angry
repetition of the concerted signal. There was a thin, bright
moonshine; it was bitter cold, windy, and frosty; the town had
not yet awakened, but an indefinable stir already preluded the
noise and business of the day. The ghouls had come later than
usual, and they seemed more than usually eager to be gone.
Fettes, sick with sleep, lighted them upstairs. He heard their
grumbling Irish voices through a dream; and as they stripped
the sack from their sad merchandise he leaned dozing,
with his shoulder propped against the wall; he had to shake
himself to find the men their money. As he did so his eyes
lighted on the dead face. He started; he took two steps nearer,
with the candle raised.

'God Almighty!' he cried. 'That is Jane Galbraith!'

The men answered nothing, but they shuffled nearer the
door.

'I know her, I tell you,' he continued. 'She was alive and hearty yesterday. It's impossible she can be dead; it's impossible you should have got this body fairly.'

'Sure, sir, you're mistaken entirely,' said one of the men.

But the other looked Fettes darkly in the eyes, and demanded the money on the spot.

It was impossible to misconceive the threat or to exaggerate the danger. The lad's heart failed him. He stammered some excuses, counted out the sum, and saw his hateful visitors depart. No sooner were they gone than he hastened to confirm his doubts. By a dozen unquestionable marks he identified the girl he had jested with the day before. He saw, with horror, marks upon her body that might well betoken violence. A panic seized him, and he took refuge in his room. There he reflected at length over the discovery that he had made; considered soberly the bearing of Mr K's instructions and the danger to himself of interference in so serious a business, and at last, in sore perplexity, determined to wait for the advice of his immediate superior, the class assistant.

This was a young doctor, Wolfe Macfarlane, a high favourite among all the reckless students, clever, dissipated, and unscrupulous to the last degree. He had travelled and studied abroad. His manners were agreeable and a little forward. He was an authority on the stage, skilful on the ice or the links with skate or golf club; he dressed with nice audacity, and, to put the finishing touch upon his glory, he kept a gig and a strong trotting-horse. With Fettes he was on terms of intimacy; indeed, their relative positions called for some community of life; and when subjects were scarce the pair would drive far into the country in Macfarlane's gig, visit and desecrate some lonely graveyard, and return before dawn with their booty to the door of the dissecting room.

On that particular morning Macfarlane arrived somewhat earlier than his wont. Fettes heard him, and met him on the stairs, told him his story, and showed him the cause of his alarm. Macfarlane examined the marks on her body.

'Yes,' he said with a nod, 'it looks fishy.'

'Well, what should I do?' asked Fettes.

'Do?' repeated the other. 'Do you want to do anything? Least said soonest mended, I should say.'

'Someone else might recognise her,' objected Fettes. 'She was as well known as the Castle Rock.'

'We'll hope not,' said Macfarlane, 'and if anybody does – well, you didn't, don't you see, and there's an end. The fact is, this has been going on too long. Stir up the mud, and you'll get K into the most unholy trouble; you'll be in a shocking box yourself. So will I, if you come to that. I should like to know how any one of us would look, or what the devil we should have to say for ourselves, in any Christian witness box. For me, you know there's one thing certain – that, practically speaking, all our subjects have been murdered.'

'Macfarlane!' cried Fettes.

'Come now!' sneered the other. 'As if you hadn't suspected it yourself!'

'Suspecting is one thing – '

'And proof another. Yes, I know; and I'm as sorry as you are this should have come here,' tapping the body with his cane. 'The next best thing for me is not to recognise it; and,' he added coolly, 'I don't. You may, if you please. I don't dictate, but I think a man of the world would do as I do; and I may add, I fancy that is what K would look for at our hands. The question is, Why did he choose us two for his assistants? And I answer, because he didn't want old wives.'

This was the tone of all others to affect the mind of a lad like Fettes. He agreed to imitate Macfarlane. The body of the unfortunate girl was duly dissected, and no one remarked or appeared to recognise her.

One afternoon, when his day's work was over, Fettes dropped into a popular tavern and found Macfarlane sitting with a stranger. This was a small man, very pale and dark, with coal-black eyes. The cut of his features gave a promise of intellect and refinement which was but feebly realised in his manners, for he proved, upon a nearer acquaintance, coarse, vulgar, and stupid. He exercised, however, a very remarkable control over Macfarlane; issued orders like the Great Bashaw; became inflamed at the least discussion or delay, and commented rudely on the servility with which he was obeyed. This most offensive person took a fancy to Fettes on the spot, plied him with drinks, and honoured him with unusual confidences on his past career. If a tenth part of what he confessed were true, he was a very loathsome rogue; and the lad's vanity was tickled by the attention of so experienced a man.

'I'm a pretty bad fellow myself,' the stranger remarked, 'but Macfarlane is the boy – Toddy Macfarlane I call him. Toddy, order your friend another glass.' Or it might be, 'Toddy, you jump up and shut the door.' 'Toddy hates me,' he said again. 'Oh yes, Toddy, you do!'

'Don't you call me that confounded name,' growled Macfarlane.

'Hear him! Did you ever see the lads play knife? He would like to do that all over my body,' remarked the stranger.

'We medicals have a better way than that,' said Fettes. 'When we dislike a dead friend of ours, we dissect him.'

Macfarlane looked up sharply, as though this jest were scarcely to his mind.

The afternoon passed. Gray, for that was the stranger's name, invited Fettes to join them at dinner, ordered a feast so sumptuous that the tavern was thrown into commotion, and when all was done commanded Macfarlane to settle the bill. It was late before they separated; the man Gray was incapably drunk. Macfarlane, sobered by his fury, chewed the cud of the money he had been forced to squander and the slights he had been obliged to swallow. Fettes, with various liquors singing in his head, returned home with devious footsteps and a mind entirely in abeyance. Next day Macfarlane was absent from the class, and Fettes smiled to himself as he imagined him still squiring the intolerable Gray from tavern to tavern. As soon as the hour of liberty had struck he posted from place to place in quest of his last night's companions. He could find them, however, nowhere; so returned early to his rooms, went early to bed, and slept the sleep of the just.

At four in the morning he was awakened by the well-known signal. Descending to the door, he was filled with astonishment to find Macfarlane with his gig, and in the gig one of those long and ghastly packages with which he was so well acquainted.

'What?' he cried. 'Have you been out alone? How did you manage?'

But Macfarlane silenced him roughly, bidding him turn to business. When they had got the body upstairs and laid it on the table, Macfarlane made at first as if he were going away. Then he paused and seemed to hesitate; and then, 'You had better look at the face,' said he, in tones of some constraint. 'You had better,' he repeated, as Fettes only stared at him in wonder.

'But where, and how, and when did you come by it?' cried the other.

'Look at the face,' was the only answer.

Fettes was staggered; strange doubts assailed him. He looked from the young doctor to the body, and then back again. At last, with a start, he did as he was bidden. He had almost expected the sight that met his eyes, and yet the shock was cruel. To see, fixed in the rigidity of death and naked on that coarse layer of sackcloth, the man whom he had left well clad and full of meat and sin upon the threshold of a tavern, awoke, even in the thoughtless Fettes, some of the terrors of the conscience. It was a *cras tibi* which re-echoed in his soul, that two whom he had known should have come to lie upon these icy tables. Yet these were only secondary thoughts. His first concern regarded Wolfe. Unprepared for a challenge so momentous, he knew not how to look his comrade in the face. He durst not meet his eye, and he had neither words nor voice at his command.

It was Macfarlane himself who made the first advance. He came up quietly behind and laid his hand gently but firmly on the other's shoulder.

'Richardson,' said he, 'may have the head.'

Now Richardson was a student who had long been anxious for that portion of the human subject to dissect. There was no answer, and the murderer resumed, 'Talking of business, you must pay me; your accounts, you see, must tally.'

Fettes found a voice, the ghost of his own: 'Pay you!' he cried. 'Pay you for that?'

'Why, yes, of course you must. By all means and on every possible account, you must,' returned the other. 'I dare not give it for nothing, you dare not take it for nothing; it would compromise us both. This is another case like Jane Galbraith's. The more things are wrong the more we must act as if all were right. Where does old K keep his money?'

'There,' answered Fettes hoarsely, pointing to a cupboard in the corner.

'Give me the key, then,' said the other, calmly, holding out his hand.

There was an instant's hesitation, and the die was cast. Macfarlane could not suppress a nervous twitch, the infinitesimal mark of an immense relief, as he felt the key between his fingers. He opened the cupboard, brought out pen and ink and a paper-book that stood in one compartment, and separated from the funds in a drawer a sum suitable to the occasion.

'Now, look here,' he said, 'there is the payment made – first proof of your good faith: first step to your security. You have now to clinch it by a second. Enter the payment in your book, and then you for your part may defy the devil.'

The next few seconds were for Fettes an agony of thought; but in balancing his terrors it was the most immediate that triumphed. Any future difficulty seemed almost welcome if he could avoid a present quarrel with Macfarlane. He set down the candle which he had been carrying all this time, and with a steady hand entered the date, the nature, and the amount of the transaction.

'And now,' said Macfarlane, 'it's only fair that you should pocket the lucre. I've had my share already. By the bye, when a man of the world falls into a bit of luck, has a few shillings extra in his pocket – I'm ashamed to speak of it, but there's a rule of conduct in the case. No treating, no purchase of expensive class-books, no squaring of old debts; borrow, don't lend.'

'Macfarlane,' began Fettes, still somewhat hoarsely, 'I have put my neck in a halter to oblige you.'

'To oblige me?' cried Wolfe. 'Oh, come! You did, as near as I can see the matter, what you downright had to do in self-defence. Suppose I got into trouble, where would you be?

This second little matter flows clearly from the first. Mr Gray is the continuation of Miss Galbraith. You can't begin and then stop. If you begin, you must keep on beginning; that's the truth. No rest for the wicked.'

A horrible sense of blackness and the treachery of fate seized hold upon the soul of the unhappy student.

'My God!' he cried, 'but what have I done? and when did I begin? To be made a class assistant – in the name of reason, where's the harm in that? Service wanted the position; Service might have got it. Would *he* have been where I am now?'

'My dear fellow,' said Macfarlane, 'what a boy you are! What harm *has* come to you? What harm *can* come to you if you hold your tongue? Why, man, do you know what this life is? There are two squads of us – the lions and the lambs. If you're a lamb, you'll come to lie upon these tables like Gray or Jane Galbraith; if you're a lion, you'll live and drive a horse like me, like K, like all the world with any wit or courage. You're staggered at the first. But look at K! My dear fellow, you're clever, you have pluck. I like you, and K likes you. You were born to lead the hunt; and I tell you, on my honour and my experience of life, three days from now you'll laugh at all these scarecrows like a High School boy at a farce.'

And with that Macfarlane took his departure and drove off up the wynd in his gig to get under cover before daylight. Fettes was thus left alone with his regrets. He saw the miserable peril in which he stood involved. He saw, with inexpressible dismay, that there was no limit to his weakness, and that, from concession to concession, he had fallen from the arbiter of Macfarlane's destiny to his paid and helpless accomplice. He would have given the world to have been a little braver at the time, but it did not occur to him that he might still be brave. The secret of Jane Galbraith and the cursed entry in the day-book closed his mouth.

Hours passed; the class began to arrive; the members of the unhappy Gray were dealt out to one and to another, and received without remark. Richardson was made happy with the head; and before the hour of freedom rang Fettes trembled with exultation to perceive how far they had already gone toward safety.

For two days he continued to watch, with increasing joy, the dreadful process of disguise.

On the third day Macfarlane made his appearance. He had been ill, he said; but he made up for lost time by the energy with which he directed the students. To Richardson in particular he extended the most valuable assistance and advice, and that student, encouraged by the praise of the demonstrator, burned high with ambitious hopes, and saw the medal already in his grasp.

Before the week was out Macfarlane's prophecy had been fulfilled. Fettes had outlived his terrors and had forgotten his baseness. He began to plume himself upon his courage, and had so arranged the story in his mind that he could look back on these events with an unhealthy pride. Of his accomplice he saw but little. They met, of course, in the business of the class; they received their orders together from Mr K. At times they had a word or two in private, and Macfarlane was from first to last particularly kind and jovial. But it was plain that he avoided any reference to their common secret; and even when Fettes whispered to him that he had cast in his lot with the lions and foresworn the lambs, he only signed to him smilingly to hold his peace.

At length an occasion arose which threw the pair once more into a closer union. Mr K was again short of subjects; pupils were eager, and it was a part of this teacher's pretensions to be always well supplied. At the same time there came the news of a burial in the rustic graveyard of Glencorse. Time has little changed the place in question. It stood then, as now, upon a cross road, out of call of human habitations, and buried fathom deep in the foliage of six cedar trees. The cries of the sheep upon the neighbouring hills, the streamlets upon either hand, one loudly singing among pebbles, the other dripping furtively from pond to pond, the stir of the wind in mountainous old flowering chestnuts, and once in seven days the voice of the bell and the old tunes of the precentor, were the only sounds that disturbed the silence around the rural church. The Resurrection Man – to use a byname of the period – was not to be deterred by any of the sanctities of customary piety. It was part of his trade to despise and desecrate the scrolls and trumpets of old tombs, the paths worn by the feet of worshippers and mourners, and the offerings and the inscriptions of bereaved affection. To rustic neighbourhoods, where love is more than commonly tenacious, and where some bonds of blood or fellowship unite the entire society of a parish, the body snatcher, far from being repelled by natural respect, was attracted by the ease and safety of the task. To bodies that had been laid in earth, in joyful expectation of a far different awakening, there came that hasty, lamp-lit, terror-haunted resurrection of the spade and mattock. The coffin was forced, the cerements torn, and the melancholy relics, clad in sackcloth, after being rattled for hours on moonless byways, were at length exposed to uttermost indignities before a class of gaping boys.

Somewhat as two vultures may swoop upon a dying lamb, Fettes and Macfarlane were to be let loose upon a grave in that green and quiet resting place. The wife of a farmer, a woman who had lived for sixty years, and been known for nothing but good butter and a godly conversation, was to be rooted from her grave at midnight and carried, dead and naked, to that far-away city that she had always honoured with her Sunday's best; the place beside her family was to be empty till the crack of doom; her innocent and almost venerable members to be exposed to that last curiosity of the anatomist.

Late one afternoon the pair set forth, well wrapped in cloaks and furnished with a formidable bottle. It rained without remission – a cold, dense, lashing rain. Now and again there blew a puff of wind, but these sheets of falling water kept it down. Bottle and all, it was a sad and silent drive as far as Penicuik, where they were to spend the evening. They stopped once, to hide their implements in a thick bush not far from the churchyard, and once again at the Fisher's Tryst, to have a toast before the kitchen fire and vary their nips of whisky with a glass of ale. When they reached their journey's end the gig was housed, the horse was fed and comforted, and the two young doctors in a private room sat down to the best dinner and the best wine the house afforded. The lights, the fire, the beating rain upon the window, the cold, incongruous work that lay before them, added zest to their enjoyment of the meal. With every glass their cordiality increased. Soon Macfarlane handed a little pile of gold to his companion.

'A compliment,' he said. 'Between friends these little d–d accommodations ought to fly like pipe-lights.'

Fettes pocketed the money, and applauded the sentiment to the echo. 'You are a philosopher,' he cried. 'I was an ass till I knew you. You and K between you, by the Lord Harry! But you'll make a man of me.'

'Of course we shall,' applauded Macfarlane. 'A man? I tell you, it required a man to back me up the other morning.

There are some big, brawling, forty-year-old cowards who would have turned sick at the look of the d–d thing; but not you – you kept your head. I watched you.'

'Well, and why not?' Fettes thus vaunted himself. 'It was no affair of mine. There was nothing to gain on the one side but disturbance, and on the other I could count on your gratitude, don't you see?' And he slapped his pocket till the gold pieces rang.

Macfarlane somehow felt a certain touch of alarm at these unpleasant words. He may have regretted that he had taught his young companion so successfully, but he had no time to interfere, for the other noisily continued in this boastful strain:

'The great thing is not to be afraid. Now, between you and me, I don't want to hang – that's practical; but for all cant, Macfarlane, I was born with a contempt. Hell, God, Devil, right, wrong, sin, crime, and all the old gallery of curiosities – they may frighten boys, but men of the world, like you and me, despise them. Here's to the memory of Gray!'

It was by this time growing somewhat late. The gig, according to order, was brought round to the door with both lamps brightly shining, and the young men had to pay their bill and take the road. They announced that they were bound for Peebles, and drove in that direction till they were clear of the last houses of the town; then, extinguishing the lamps, returned upon their course, and followed a by-road toward Glencorse. There was no sound but that of their own passage, and the incessant, strident pouring of the rain. It was pitch dark; here and there a white gate or a white stone in the wall guided them for a short space across the night; but for the most part it was at a foot pace, and almost groping, that they picked their way through that resonant blackness to their solemn and isolated destination. In the sunken woods that

94

traverse the neighbourhood of the burying ground the last glimmer failed them, and it became necessary to kindle a match and re-illumine one of the lanterns of the gig. Thus, under the dripping trees, and environed by huge and moving shadows, they reached the scene of their unhallowed labours.

They were both experienced in such affairs, and powerful with the spade; and they had scarce been twenty minutes at their task before they were rewarded by a dull rattle on the coffin lid. At the same moment Macfarlane, having hurt his hand upon a stone, flung it carelessly above his head. The grave, in which they now stood almost to the shoulders, was close to the edge of the plateau of the graveyard; and the gig lamp had been propped, the better to illuminate their labours, against a tree, and on the immediate verge of the steep bank descending to the stream. Chance had taken a sure aim with the stone. Then came a clang of broken glass; night fell upon them; sounds alternately dull and ringing announced the bounding of the lantern down the bank, and its occasional collision with the trees. A stone or two, which it had dislodged in its descent, rattled behind it into the profundities of the glen; and then silence, like night, resumed its sway; and they might bend their hearing to its utmost pitch, but naught was to be heard except the rain, now marching to the wind, now steadily falling over miles of open country.

They were so nearly at an end of their abhorred task that they judged it wisest to complete it in the dark. The coffin was exhumed and broken open; the body inserted in the dripping sack and carried between them to the gig; one mounted to keep it in its place, and the other, taking the horse by the mouth, groped along by wall and bush until they reached the wider road by the Fisher's Tryst. Here was a faint, diffused radiancy, which they hailed like daylight; by that they pushed the horse to a good pace and began to rattle along merrily in the direction of the town.

They had both been wetted to the skin during their operations, and now, as the gig jumped among the deep ruts, the thing that stood propped between them fell now upon one and now upon the other. At every repetition of the horrid contact each instinctively repelled it with the greater haste; and the process, natural although it was, began to tell upon the nerves of the companions. Macfarlane made some ill-favoured jest about the farmer's wife, but it came hollowly from his lips, and was allowed to drop in silence. Still their unnatural burden bumped from side to side; and now the head would be laid, as if in confidence, upon their shoulders, and now the drenching sackcloth would flap icily about their faces. A creeping chill began to possess the soul of Fettes. He peered at the bundle, and it seemed somehow larger than at first. All over the countryside, and from every degree of distance, the farm dogs accompanied their passage with tragic ululations; and it grew and grew upon his mind that some unnatural miracle had been accomplished, that some nameless change had befallen the dead body, and that it was in fear of their unholy burden that the dogs were howling.

'For God's sake,' said he, making a great effort to arrive at speech, 'for God's sake, let's have a light!'

Seemingly Macfarlane was affected in the same direction; for, though he made no reply, he stopped the horse, passed the reins to his companion, got down, and proceeded to kindle the remaining lamp. They had by that time got no farther than the crossroad down to Auchenclinny. The rain still poured as though the deluge were returning, and it was no easy matter to make a light in such a world of wet and darkness. When at last the flickering blue flame had been transferred to the wick and began to expand and clarify, and shed a wide circle of misty brightness round the gig, it became possible for the two young men to see each other and the thing they had along with them. The rain had moulded the rough sacking to the outlines of the body underneath; the head was distinct from the trunk, the shoulders plainly modelled; something at once spectral and human riveted their eyes upon the ghastly comrade of their drive.

For some time Macfarlane stood motionless, holding up the lamp. A nameless dread was swathed, like a wet sheet, about the body, and tightened the white skin upon the face of Fettes; a fear that was meaningless, a horror of what could not be, kept mounting to his brain. Another beat of the watch, and he had spoken. But his comrade forestalled him.

'That is not a woman,' said Macfarlane, in a hushed voice.

'It was a woman when we put her in,' whispered Fettes.

'Hold that lamp,' said the other. 'I must see her face.'

And as Fettes took the lamp his companion untied the fastenings of the sack and drew down the cover from the head. The light fell very clear upon the dark, well-moulded features and smooth-shaven cheeks of a too familiar countenance, often beheld in dreams of both of these young men. A wild yell rang up into the night; each leaped from his own side into the roadway: the lamp fell, broke, and was extinguished; and the horse, terrified by this unusual commotion, bounded and went off toward Edinburgh at a gallop, bearing along with it, sole occupant of the gig, the body of the dead and long-dissected Gray.

Robert Louis Stevenson was born in Edinburgh in 1850. Both his father and his grandfather were successful and prominent engineers, and Robert intended to follow in their footsteps, but was prevented by the early onset of tuberculosis. For much of his childhood he was confined to bed through ill health, and passed his time reading and writing stories, and this early apprenticeship, together with his constant travelling in search of a healthier climate, provided much material for his later writing. Conversely Stevenson's rejection of the religious doctrine and Victorian ethics he was taught as a bedridden child was at once a cause of his subsequent uneasy relationship with his father, and a frequent theme in his mature literature.

At the age of seventeen, Stevenson entered Edinburgh University, where he studied law, without much enthusiasm, and where his first pieces were published in university journals. In 1875 he was called to the Scottish Bar, but decided against practising law in favour of writing. He continued to publish small pieces in journals, and in 1878 and 1879 his first full-length travel writings, *An Inland Voyage* and *Travels with a Donkey in the Cévennes*, were published. It was whilst in France that Stevenson met and fell in love with Fanny Vandegrift Osbourne, a married American. When she returned to her husband in California, Stevenson set off from Scotland to find her, and after arriving dangerously ill and penniless, he finally persuaded her to obtain a divorce. They were married in 1880, and returned to Britain the same year.

In 1883 Stevenson achieved his first major literary success with the adventure story *Treasure Island*, and many of his best-known works were produced during the following few years, including *A Child's Garden of Verses* (1885), *Kidnapped*

(1886), and *Dr Jekyll and Mr Hyde* (1886). Stevenson's works, though critical of the straitening Victorian value system within which he lived, were nevertheless deeply moral works, and in critical essays published at this time, Stevenson rejected the European trend towards Realism, maintaining that humans were essentially noble.

While his career began to burgeon, Stevenson's health nevertheless remained precarious, and in 1888, following the death of his father, he and his family set off for the South Pacific. In 1890, realising that a return to Scotland was now impossible in view of Stevenson's health, they settled permanently in Samoa. Stevenson wrote many sympathetic essays and letters on the subject of South-Seas culture, and campaigned for self-rule for the islanders. He continued to produce fiction, too, and many novels and short stories, including *Island Nights' Entertainments* (1893), and *The Ebb-Tide* (1894), reflected his time in Samoa. Stevenson finally died of a stroke in December 1894, and was buried at the top of Mount Vaea in Samoa.

HESPERUS PRESS CLASSICS

Hesperus Press, as suggested by the Latin motto, is committed to bringing near what is far – far both in space and time. Works written by the greatest authors, and unjustly neglected or simply little known in the English-speaking world, are made accessible through new translations and a completely fresh editorial approach. Through these classic works, the reader is introduced to the greatest writers from all times and all cultures.

For more information on Hesperus Press, please visit our website: **www.hesperuspress.com**

ET REMOTISSIMA PROPE